KILLA

NONFICTION BY MARIO MORENO

*The Pocket Screenwriting Guide: 120 Tips for Getting to
FADE OUT*
(with Anthony Grieco) @PktScreenGD
Column: scriptmag.com/author/mariomoreno
Guest column: savethecat.com/author/mario-moreno

MARIO MORENO'S
KILLA

A MIXTAPE NOVELLA

NEON CAT

A NEON CAT MIXTAPE NOVELLA
KILLA: A Mixtape Novella by Mario Moreno
Published by Neon Cat Content
A division of Neon Cat, LLC
www.NeonCatContent.com

Workshopped in Andrew Guerdat's Writers Group
Edited by Kerry Cullen
Proofread by Michele Gendelman
Interior Design and Typesetting by Damonza
Cover by Fernando Reza (Fro Design Studio)
Typography inspired by Lack76 and Tanker
Neon Cat logo by Pabitra Hader
Logo based on a design by May Phan
Author photo by Maria Real

Library of Congress Control Number: 2022919147

ISBN 979-8-9867999-9-5 (hardcover)
ISBN 979-8-9867999-8-8 (audiobook)
ISBN 979-8-9867999-7-1 (paperback)
ISBN 979-8-9867999-6-4 (ebook)

First Edition
2 4 6 8 9 7 5 3 1

For you

"If I am the phantom, it is because man's hatred has made me so."

—LE FANTÔME DE L'OPÉRA, GASTON LEROUX

"Candidly, my strategy's like Eric B. & Rakim's
On 'My Melody'
Incapacity—savagely—calamity—rapidly
Hurricane, Heavy rain, that's my malady
How I became, how Heavy reign
How I'll remain Your Pure Majesty"

—HEAVY REIGN (REMIX), KING HEAVY

ঙ Playlist ♡

Track 1

Killa
(Intro)

AYO, MUSE, GONNA sing one for *you*—
gonna spit bars of truth, broadcasting from afar,
unmasking the view by spinning a playlist
dishing on the dawn when the monster was created,
and the villains, and the heroine,
and the broken night of the vengeance—
check it:

As the alligators closed in on him in the pre-sun swamp,
young Apocalypse—man of his words, the prince of a
    Latin King,
the hip-hop ghostwriter seeking to seed generational wealth,
like Odysseus, for his baby and his girl—*his ladies*—

and his family up north still struggling themselves—
that Apocalypse—the former banger and tagger from
    the Bronx,
haggard performer battered and splattered numb on the
    Miami rocks,
responsible for the star, the show, the flow, the whole
    thing—the man—
couldn't stop remembering
how earlier that night he'd watched as the beat dropped,
his lines delivered by Heavy—rough,
the rapper rhyming Apocalypse's lines on the right side
of the bright lights, working the crowd sweaty,
brows like hurricane levees, cult-like rain from the heavens.
Verbs, other words, and earworms bought and resold by the
    local legend
on the vintage vocals transmitter (a satin chrome-plated, die-
    cast-cased Shure 55SH mic)
as Apocalypse, the striver, the dreamer, the underesti-
    mated scribe,
the one the gods had fated and faded,
spied the show from the shadows, proud voyeur waiting—
sound drowned out, world in slow motion,
an ocean of flashing lights storming in his pupils by the oodles,
purple and gold. Verbals encircled, curdled, and retold.
Eyeing the world from the wings was teaching him
    things useful.

Apocalypse's nostrils flared at the scent of beer, weed,
AC, fog machines, pheromones, cigarettes, and sweat
in the creepy old playhouse with the proscenium stage.
Wurlitzer pipe organ. Marble frame around the arch.

Red curtains lit by lasers and strobes. Miami partying
like it was 1999— because it was.
The whole place charged, rocking with the rhythm
of 500 drinking, rolling, and smoking B-boys, B-girls, and
    rump-shakers
moving in unison to the show onstage:

King Heavy, smooth operator, player's player,
strutting on the mic in drenched black jeans and tee,
flashing gold
as the sound came alive for Apocalypse,
and the mo was no longer slow.
His song getting dropped by the deep voice of the legend,
and homie wasn't even thirty.
    "I manifest the best, fresha than the rest
    Digits fulla rings, when I touch bitches
    They sing"

Apocalypse studied Heavy owning the masses, in the dark.
Dying to taste that adoration, hungry for recognition.
Heavy glanced at him, the king's face a Rubik's cube of
gel-colored lights and strobing hues. Winked. Turned to
    his fans:
    "Tell the rest of the pests to give it a rest
    Heavy's the King - surely, y'all jest, stressed
    What y'all willin' to do for success?"
Apocalypse mouthing along:
    "Heavy throwin' up that Miami set
    Don't y'all ever fuckin' forget"
Hold up. Apocalypse stopped.
That wasn't the end line he wrote, that wasn't the flow.

Apocalypse knew it all by rote, by heart, like blood;
didn't need to check his rhyme book,
and didn't need a degree—except from the streets—
to know King Heavy, aka Bettino White, didn't do anything
     by accident.
Disrespected.
Diss reflected in the prior lines the king had euthanized.
This expected, but still stinging—unexpected—after all this
     time, Apocalypse still affected.

Heavy dropped the mic.
Formed an "M" with thumbs and forefingers,
raised his hands. His flock matched him like mirrors.
Heavy bowed. And the disciples went fucking wild.
The king stayed onstage to bask in the applause.
But Apocalypse couldn't get past the corruption
of his lyrics. Even though the house had been brought down.
Even though the roof (and chandelier rigged with speakers)
     had officially been raised.
Furious—still, Apocalypse felt compelled to keep
     his composure,
but hearing alarm clocks in his thoughts. Ringtones saying:
Something's Gotta Give like the Beastie Boys' psalm.
Apocalypse had waited long enough. Time to show his stuff.
     Prove himself up to snuff.
Not about to give up.
That's what's up.
Those were Apocalypse's memories as the alligators advanced,
     and his recollections went on…

Thinking on how thirty-seven minutes and twelve seconds   100
    after the show,
he'd lit a spiked blunt, sitting solo in the backseat of a '96
    Explorer.
Ozium spray scent overcome by the illicit chimichurri,
hot-boxing the SUV, he two-toked the herb
and passed to Nicole Echo-No-Mics [pronounced *Economics*],
"Nicole" for short, "Echo,"-multi-hyphen for official,
shorty at the wheel; the queen bee who made things happen
for other people. One eye fixed on her pager, a perma-
    nent feature.   110
Dope as the smoke was, Apocalypse didn't notice,
too focused dissecting grievances from his list:
            "The last line's supposed to be 'Bet'—
            like 'You can bet on it'
            or 'Bet that up, I owe you one.'"
        "I know, hon."
            "Anyone can say, 'Don't y'all ever fuckin' forget.'
            Where's the art? He always be simplifyin' the flow.
            Shit, it ain't 1899, Nicole."
        "I feel ya, hon. I really do.   120
        Full club, all them heads cheering,
        promoters paying, merch selling out.
        Clearly, Heavy doesn't know shit
        about rocking a crowd."
            "Stop playin'."
        "Why's he gotta go and simplify your rhymes, right?
        It's not like he's the one on stage—vibing, grooving,
        communing with the peeps, or nothing like that."
            "Nah, you right, E. Airtight. I'm bein' a bitch.
            He's a star.   130

5

That's why it's time for me to step up,
          or bellyflop."
     "We just done spoke about this, Lips.
     You gotta think about the business—"
               "I gotta jump. Get to making my own music. Fast.
               Drop the top on a time machine and catch up."
Nicole Echo-No-Mics, the pragmatist diplomat,
the sister-like sister, Heavy's actual sister, turned
to Apocalypse, her hair silver-dyed. She exhaled,
careful not to spill ashes on her white jeans and halter top,   140
Santería necklaces resting atop her glistening, beating heart;
Apocalypse's gaze accidentally lingered on her cleavage—
not cheating, but Echo-No-Mics was cute-to-hot—
even though her eyes were barbed.
          "You said it yourself:
          He's the star.
          Do the knowledge.
          What's best for you?"
Fed up, Apocalypse glanced out the tinted window
at the renovated Deco theater-turned-nightspot, after-hours   150
     line down the block.
NEON SIGNS above the door and on the roof throwing up
     their sets

"CLUB VALDEMAR"
while in the car, Nicole was like:
          "One day soon, when you're hot shit,
          you can fuck up someone else's rhymes."
               "When's that gonna be, Nicole? Ain't
               you supposed to be my manager, too?"
          "Why I'm telling you, let me handle it."   160
Her pager BEEPED. She pulled the whip around—

past lowriders cruising and racers revving turbo—
to the stage door behind the theater, like a budget limousine.
        "Timing's a delicate bitch."

But Apocalypse knew all about time. After all, he'd loved
    hip-hop,
since before his balls dropped. Most of his 27. When his voice
    was still high,
his Ma and Pops played him Sugarhill Gang, Treacherous
    Three, Funky Four + 1, Furious Five   170
on the radio as much as rock, Steely Dan, and pop.
When Mattingly was the Yankees' leader, years before Jeter.
Before Apocalypse's Pops got shot—POP, POP, POP!

Years later, Apocalypse the prince did a stint, on the same path
    as his dad,
up in Rikers—frantically writing rhymes in his bunk late
    at night,
and on from dawn once it arrived—awakened.
In turn, taking the fam to Miami, nerves shaking.
Home of Luke and 2 Live Crew, Poison Clan-affiliated—   180
true heroes for the former banger looking for a better handle.
Baby momma humming with a demo in her embryo.

But sunny beaches burned Apocalypse
with other lessons learned over time.
#1, the American Dream was mostly lies. Unwise
to leave slanging and banging
behind in the Bronx—at least it seemed.

Then he was befriended by an up-and-comer called
    King Heavy—
beguiled by his charms, ease, and assurances.   190
The king, teasing encouragement, swore to Apocalypse
he'd serve his demo to the Fates of the Biz,
instead of the fakes and haters trying to play him like the Wiz,
    jacking percentages—
if Apocalypse paid dues, stayed in the backdrop first, wrote for
    Heavy in the front.
King got what he wanted. Then he cut Apocalypse out of
    the clams,
leaving him and the fam eating chorizo lentil soup made
    with Spam.   200

Apocalypse looked at himself now, in the tinted back-
    seat window
of Nicole's Explorer. Club Valdemar in the background. Plans
    hadn't worked
out. Writing rhymes like a ghost, golden-egg laying goose,
plans slaughtered like a cow, shit fulla bull, milked dry,
turned to feed, a cog in the machine, meat already rotten.
Dreams that he and his girl had for them and their baby
forgotten—pen in his hand, begging like he's homeless,
hoping for a handout, praying   210
for a miracle, lacking faith—exhausted from the wait.
Apocalypse exhaled from his thoughts.
In the laced Northern Lights smoke, remembrances resembling
    the sketch of his chemtrails.
He reached into his pocket, pulled out a copy
of the demo he'd recorded in secret from Heavy,
over Nicole's blessing, letting out what he'd been holding in:

"Gonna tell Heavy at the after-party."
Nicole tried to snatch the tape out of Apocalypse's hand,
    all like: 220
        "Don't be crazy. Do no such thing—"
Heavy slid into shotgun, smelling of the stage,
smoke seeping out like from a hookah lounge in the clouds.
Apocalypse concealed the tape,
cursed himself as Heavy shut the door—
hype-men, homies, and honeys, falling away.
    "Let's roll. Get the fuck outta here.
    Need to cop a new whip, Nicole. Kings
    can't be seen riding in fuckin' nine-six Explorers."
Apocalypse tabled the convo, off the glance Nicole gave him;   230
stared down at his black Tim-boots and yellow laces,
kicking himself
for fearing blowing up his shot by speaking his thoughts,
tell-offs for Heavy on the tip of his tongue
as the Explorer pulled away from the club.
Miami pissed rain on the windshield, red and teal streaks.
On the itinerary: hit up a couple after-parties,
then Steve's Pizza or Miami Subs, break night
before getting dropped off. Go to sleep post-dawn, still kicking
himself beside his girl, headphones on, bumping   240
DJ Craze or Uncle Al into his ear canals,
hoping the Miami bass will drown out the pain.
Apocalypse wrapped up in his mixtape of thoughts.
Heavy didn't waste any time, asked:
    "Finish them raps for me, dawg?"
Going with the flow, like an emcee knowing his role,
Apocalypse handed Heavy a bundle
of heartbreak, hope, and perseverance in the form of flows

weighing sixteen ounces of flesh, cosmic energy
in a NOTEBOOK tag-titled:

"HEAVY REIGN!
Album Lyrics"

Heavy flipped through pages of rhymes
in neat graffiti. Moving his lips, seeing the lines
for the first time. Sage stanzas, scribbled in Sharpie,
extending into the margins. Subtle murmurs of approval
to himself. Shut it. Heavy shifted the topic
once he seemed to get what he wanted:
    "Peep the demo Slick was bumpin'
    at the Fade House."
Heavy offered up a tape:

"KILLA" tagged on one side,
"Apocalypse" on the other.

Apocalypse saw the writing—
heard Nicole starting up the same string as him, like:
    "We were gonna tell you."
Her daggers locked in on Apocalypse in the rear view.
The prince *knowing* she *knew* he was the *one*
who slipped it to a mutual acquaintance
known for gossiping, like the Ancients, with no hesitation.
Glaring at him like he must've compromised him-
    self intentionally
to slip the Freudian. Seeking dramatic static to get past it,
a confrontation to bring the issue to a head.

Apocalypse would've sworn he hadn't but doubted the answer.
Heavy like:
    "All good in the hood.
    Sound the trumpets, playas.
    Ain't got all night."
He held up the tape, made Nicole do the deed. She popped
the demo in the deck. Pressed "Play." Nodded to the BEAT
that BOOMED from her woofers and subwoofers.
The song, a post Golden Age banger, epic beat
with eerie GRAND PIANOS and sound effects of JETS;
the lyrics straight from Apocalypse, his voice
coming over the speakers,
two 12s in the back, four 8s in the cabin:
        "Sick of the sidelines, I gotta get mine
        Shine - divine mind for our times, my advice
        To the gentlemen, ladies, and babies"
The king listened close.
Stereo-deck lights leveled-up and down the EQ,
bass and treble, and the middle,
with a bounce for the ounce, radio
bulbs and timbre synced to the tempo—
Apocalypse's voice fulla soul and swing, like:
        "Be an emcee killa
        Before an emcee kill ya
        Do you in for a label
        That can't feel or see ya
        Kill an emcee where it hurts
        Soft underbelly in the megahertz
        Beat a drum with hooks and bars
        Stab a song in the back, no love"
Heavy smiled.

So they all smiled.
Chilling, just taking it in.
Nicole mimed a drum loop like she looped it.
As Apocalypse's voice kept on booming:
> *"Killa born and reborn an orphan*
> *Dying to pull good from bad*
> *Like a rabbit from a trap, top hat, or a coffin*
> *Emcee dreams be all a killa ever had*
> *Writing rhymes since I started coughin'*
> *Lying for a rhyme scheme, truth be, no later than*
> > *age nine*
> *Now equipped with rhymes for all times*
> *and All Time*
> *—all kinds—*
> *'Cuz it's my time*
> *My time*
> *My time*
> *To design, build and fill shrines"*

Embracing fate,
Apocalypse rhymed along with the lines to his song,
jugular on his sleeve, exposing it to his mentor—his boss,
the legend, the opinion that mattered, H, the king, the
    Heavy One,
until they got to the end, and Nicole joined in:
> *"'Cuz I'm an emcee killa,*
> *I'm an emcee killa*
> *ain't none reala - ain't none illa*
> *I'm an emcee killa"*

The Killa chorus staccato.
Over stabbing strings—cellos, violins—
sampled out of an old suspense flick—

using the space between the notes,
background vocals sung by *his girl*, a natural,
then ending on an ode to Wu and Ol' Dirty:
a long-sung note—gotta clear the sample.
Sounding like a debut single.

Heavy nodded, gregarious aura: 340
    "Killa—with a capital A."

Apocalypse leaned forward
between the front seats, said to the king:
            "With your sister's brains and our tracks,
            we could rise up out the hood for good.
            Bring up a crew, be like Wu-Tang or Boot Camp,
            you know, bro—like Big said, 'Sky's the limit—'"
Heavy SHUT OFF the demo.
Filled the silence with a question:
    "Know why Pac got shot?"   350
            "What?"
    "Bet Suge was behind it. Just like errbody thinks.
    Makes sense. How else he finna do it with the spotlight?"
Apocalypse was thrown by the sudden change of topic.
Heavy going on:
    "Maybe he deserved it. Maybe Pac suddenly thought
    he didn't need his homie. Thought he could venture off
    solo and say fuck errbody else. Outlaw."

Apocalypse leaned back, stared forward.
Sensed Nicole tense too. All quiet. Heavy like: 360
    "Turn here."

Nicole steered onto 95, the expressway a surprise and dark in
    those parts.
Wrong turn, Apocalypse calling it out:
            "The after-party's—"
"We headed to a better one. No doubt."
Heavy sniffed, belligerent, a click in his mind apparent.
        Apocalypse forgot all about the blunt in his hand
burning down to long ash.
                "There ain't nothing Pac could do that was   370
                    so bad."
Apocalypse heard a GUN COCKED. Heavy turned
back in his seat, pressed his .45 Glock to the emcee kil-
    la's mouth,
the king telling more than asking:
    "No?"
Apocalypse looked to Nicole, but she kept her eyes on
    the road.
    "And gimme that fuckin' stank."

Oxygen repugnant,   380
choking on the sodden smell
of a sulfur-methane cocktail,
Everglades, rotten eggs, reptile carcasses
as the Explorer's high beams illuminated the swamp,
permeating red mangroves in the predawn fog.
Apocalypse never envisioned it would come to this—
exiled to the Glades before the crack of day, off Alligator Alley,
middle-of-nowhere in the slumbering world—pondering the
    odds of survival,
how he would return to his baby and his girl.   390

Could it be a test? Heavy learning him a lesson, teaching him
    by leaning on him?
Apocalypse contemplating, hoping—forced out into the wild
    at Glock-point,
pleading to Nicole Echo-No Mics,
greeted by silence, like the poor by Reaganomics—
as Heavy CLOCKED him with the butt of his gun.

Apocalypse fell
into marshland, shocked, stunned. On his knees, bleeding.
Felt the warmth of liquid dripping onto his cheek. Saw drop-
    lets dilute in the bog.
Humidity Hell. Fabric sticking to him. Skin infected
    with toxins.
Spirit hurting. Body near numb. Symphony of insects, Mozart
    mosquitos with oboe stingers.
Nicole finally stepped up, stepped between them on the edge
    of the swamp:
      "You made your point, Bettino.
      Let's roll. You two are a team,
      thicker than fam. This is some ghetto-
      ass shit. We're better than this."
Heavy spit at Apocalypse like:
      "Little bitch ain't better than shit."
Nicole took another tack:
      "He'll never be better than you, bro,
      no doubt, now or forever. You know
      no one ever will. So, let's let it go. Start over."
      "Ain't no doubts already, Nicole.
      Don't you worry 'bout nothing at all, dawg."
        "Good, let's help him up."

Heavy paused her from the task, Glock still in his hand.
  "The king graced this bitch's limericks
  with his presence, and this is what the king gets?
  Stabbed in the back by a wack rapper?
  Another pretender to the throne?"
Heavy talking about himself in third person—
a tell when he felt threatened.
Apocalypse's hurt and shock turned to anger,
the dormant gangster awakened, manhood
challenged, called out, channeled back,
prepared to pounce. Apocalypse felt his face
carve a bloody smile, defiant:
          "Wack?"
He spat blood.
          "I birthed you, bitch."
Heavy like:
  "Hear this fool, Nicole?"
Nicole like:
          "Stop playing, both of y'all.
          We fam. Let's sleep on it and
          spit in the morn."
Apocalypse tried to rise. Heavy kicked him
back down to the bog, ottoman chucked aside.
Brandishing his copy of the track, Heavy
stepped closer:
  "Who in the fuck gave you permission
  to go out and make a fuckin' demo?"
Heavy kicked the prince while he was down.
Apocalypse ate marsh, said:
          "Just 'cuz I been makin' your lunch
          for lifetimes don't mean I ain't got the right

to fuckin' eat."
Apocalypse rose. Heavy flipped
the Glock around, NAILED him
with it again—THWACK!
Heavy like:
    "You eat when the king says
    you eat, bitch."
Nicole like:
        "We're gonna rake twice as much bank
        with you two working together."
    "Only room for fuckin' one."
            "Who says it gots to be you?"
    "Royal decree, bitch."
Heavy Glock-whipped him again—
SNAP! Apocalypse felt his head fall back,
woozy, view of the predawn blurry,
cotton-ball clouds far from 20/20.
His dazed gaze drifted up to Nicole,
who had tears in hers. Sky full of stars.
        "C'mon, bro—he's got a girl
        and a kid. Stop tripping."
Heavy like:
    "Hold this fool down."
        "For what? Enough already—"
    "The king said hold this fool down."
        "Forget it, 'king,' 'H', fucking Bettino, bro—
        whatever name you wanna be called.
        You don't wanna work with him? Fine.
        You don't need him. Just let him go—"
    "Don't make me tell you again, Nicole."
Apocalypse like:

"Can't never… do shit…
        for your…self."
Heavy kicked his mouth; Apocalypse felt teeth pop out—
speechless, as if his speech left—
saw Heavy glare at Nicole. *Now.*

Nicole gripped each wrist. Pinned them
down as Apocalypse tried to resist.
Some wiring gone lose in his head. Broken. Struggling   490
    to process
how low the so-called "king" would go to own
    Apocalypse's flow.
Overwhelmed with a bevy of regrets,
to-do-lists of do-overs under examination, filling his
    brain's container,
hemorrhaging, gushing, reeling from revelations, repenting
    Heavy relations.
Missing his lady and their baby.
Wishing he was home with them, his saviors.   500
Might rig the antenna, try to catch shut-eye
to Saturday Night Funk Box with DJ Rhythm Rocka on 88.9.
Girl in his arms, baby in the crib. Cassette radio on "Record."
Righteous way to live.
Asking himself: *"Why did I get my ass in this mess?"*
But it's fruitless.
Starting to rain. Cold drops
slapping his face, disgraced. Their beat the soundtrack to
    his pain.
Silent heat lightning flashed in the distance, thunder too far to   510
    be heard.
Heavy hovered over him, taunting:

"You got your own flow, huh, dawg?"
He produced a LONG KNIFE
and PLIERS.
     "Ever hear of Hammurabi's Code?"

Apocalypse's view went wide,
then narrowed to the threat.
He struggled to free himself. Saw Nicole horrified—eyes fixed
     on knife and pliers:
          "What the shit you doing, bro?"
     "Not now, Nicole."
          "Don't do this, Bettino."
     "Quiet the fuck up!"
Heavy said, then returned focus to Apocalypse.
     "Eye for an eye?
     You know it.
     You a well-read muh-fucka.
     Well, it goes on: a
     tooth for a tooth… a
     tongue for a tongue…"
               "Betta fuckin' kill me, dawg.
               And my ghost. Swear to God,
               I'ma fuckin' haunt you—"
Apocalypse struggled, got one arm free,
DEFLECTED the BLADE—
right at Nicole's face—
it SLICED across her cheek
like a nasty zipper—
Nicole SHRIEKED, looked away—
but Apocalypse knew she heard *his* SCREAM—
which was suffocated by an excruciating tug,

resistance worthless, wasted, a severing—
no severance,
then weightlessness—
a RUSTY CARVING SOUND—
LOUD, GURGLY—and
—*RIP!*—
a TEARING—
followed by bloody,							550
muted
suction,
WHEEZING and CRYING; Apocalypse
feeling his throat choking on itself,
thick liquid, taste the blood spout,
honey lava molasses, sun-smoldering hot,
then numb—last felt filling his lungs
as Heavy rose, holding Apocalypse's
jagged tongue
like a trophy dripping guts,						560
voice box—larynx—strings loose,
sinuous. Way Apocalypse knew
the nightmare was cold truth.
Nicole, doused with it, too—
voice cracking, breaking, crying out:
   "Sweet Jesus!"
Apocalypse could hear his life flashing
behind his ears.

    "Shank a track, drop an album
    Hang a harmony riff in a yard				570
    'Gonna pull strings' - pulling your strings
    Suffocate ya with: 'Gonna make ya a star'
    Bragging 'bout being a 'god emcee,

gonna make ya just like me'*
Exterminate ya whole discography
Scratched record, a hole left where your soul went
Leave ya all for dead, silent dread
Muted six feet under the mix,
Dirt deep, where no one can hear ya from a
    permanent bed—   580
mastered, remixed, or remastered
Bastard
Executioner emcee, serious as a samurai soldier
Apocalypse from an esophagus, assassinate a line
Told ya
Emcees rhymin' 'bout themselves in third person
I'm first, talkin' to you in second"

Jolted out of his silhouette-soliloquy thoughts, Apocalypse
heard Heavy ripping off his chorus,
adding insult: 590
    "I'm an emcee killa,
I'm an emcee killa -
ain't none reala.
Stupid."
Heavy tossed the tongue into the swamp—

                    PLOP!

Holding her torn cheek, blood seeping, Nicole crossed herself
in the rain as Heavy said:
    "Now the gators know breakfast is ready.
Play 'em that wack-ass demo,   600
see if it charts."

Under the pitchfork downpour, young Apocalypse—

the dreamer, the striver, the underestimated scribe,
the one the gods had faded and fated—
replayed his loss, feeling a fool, ashamed—
heard a HISS,
forced open his swollen eyes. Glimpsed
rustling grass, glowing cherry orbs
on the dampened surface of the night,
shimmering across a rippling glass sea like dawn suns,   610
enshrouded by fog,
a galaxy of ruby disco-mirror balls.
Life proven a harlot, Nas proven right—
Apocalypse saw what they were:
Alligator periscopes,
slit irises, pupils dead-set, intense scarlet,
emerging from the red marshes, puncturing the wet darkness.

Heavy spoke to the gators
like the predators were players waiting:
"Who got next?"   620

The Miseducation of Pretty-Dope

MELODY'S EYES SNAP open—
tense, tired, shifting back and forth,
stung by salt, blinded by a spotlight.
Her emcee ambitions on the ropes.
Pretty-smart, pretty-cool, pretty-dope,
and Pretty-Dope's what she goes by when she flows.
Somewhere between Lauryn Hill and Cardi B.
Wiser than her 23—or so she thinks.
Right now, her lips are frozen.
Laceless shell-tops on her feet, one tapping: a tic. 10

Her eyes dart to an ELECTRIC CLOCK
offstage, ticking down: 45 seconds…
Its twin behind her, a background backdrop like a metro-
	nome timebomb…
The BREAK-BEAT baits her.
She nods, trying to catch a flow.
A KICK and a SNARE waiting for her to ride them…
King Heavy, her hero, in attendance,
intimidating anticipation.
The audience grows restless. 43, 42, 41…
Jeers seep through:
	"Who the fuck is you, bitch?!"
Aimed at Melody—Mel for short—
the one desiring R-E-S-P-E-C-T like Aretha, trying to lasso a
	style she calls Drunken Meter—
that's the M-E-T-H-O-D—like Bruce Lee's water:
sometimes it rhymes like a poem,
and sometimes it's prose that doesn't.
But the liquid's lost in the ether, spigot's closed.
Divine nectar in the negative, ledger in the red.
37, 36, 35, 34…
The countdown reflects in her eyes—
can see it, and herself—
frozen in a nightmare…

❧

Seems like, even in her dreams, she's stuck.
That's all Mel can remember at dawn
in La Dulce Vista's staff bathroom.
On another Labor Day in butt-fuck.
Staring in the mirror, holding

a mic—no, a toothbrush.
Still frozen.
Cursed, always going back and forth on her own decisions
until the actions themselves become insignificant.
Itchy in maid's polyester, she gazes at her tired reflection.
Labor Day's no holiday for her.
Can't go nowhere; double shift declared on short notice.
Working 9-to-5 and 5-to-9, the real
gig economy. Shit more like a triple.
    "Be thankful," Mima said earlier,
    "that it's not another multiple."
One way or another, the dealio since Abuelita's been gone.
No more sandwiches Cubano or Pan con Lechón.
Can't even afford a couple croquettas. Added insult
to their loss. Their lives reeking of laundromats and
    litter boxes.
On the holiday heels of a graveyard shift, Mel sneaking a
    break. Sick of it.
Qué clase de vida es esta—
living off continental breakfast scraps at La Dulce Vista?
Huh?
Servant to sun-drunk tourists. Stench of sunblock and
    wet towels.
Mel the tender alto's tenure keeping Mima above water,
like a good daughter.
The grind more like indentured servitude,
troubled by absence of legal tender. Lack of funds
sweeping horizons farther, freedom a non-starter.
Conceiving of being a star with clout—
more likely to dwarf, recede, and burn out.
Rich soaring, but more important: the poor

getting sorer. Need to get it sorted. Recently saw
Mima riding Greg the Boss's sword in the office—
him in his chair, her on his lap, Jordans
pressed against the floor, door open,
sort of like before, gored by other bosses' horns—
to survive, to provide, too ambitious to think about thriving
—bruises buried—tales all sordid—
overtures leaving Mima and Mel with nothing, vibes distorted,
    goddamn Central Florida.
Raw deal, but for real: tempting to lie, cheat and steal.   80
Lost in the, lost in the, lost in the Clorox haze
of the long day,
preaching to the chorus.
Tired reflection egging her on, Mel
grabs a bar of soap, draws
a goatee on her face; graffiti
from her brain, teeth blacked out,
an arrow through her head, leaving
her defaced. Vandalized. Barely able to hold her own eyes.
Doesn't like what she sees in her stare.   90
Something going on there.
So she turns to her phone. Planning to bottomless scroll,
cleaning up after bottomless mimosas.
But she spots an alert. Calls up the
NittyGrittyMiamiHipHop app.
A VIDEO STREAMS ON SCREEN:
starring Polynesian American Truth-Is,
underground reporter, mover, shaker.
Her thrift style an influence
on Mel, who wonders what the truth is for Truth-Is.   100
Tries to imagine what her life's like—

not just the big city and the lights,
but what a room—that's not a closet for brooms—is like.
Miami Beach condo in the background of her vid,
the opposite of gloom. Fancy fins showcasing an aquarium
while Mel's tiny twisted-tail Tosakin goldfish, Miles Davis,
lives in a hand-me-down bowl in Mel's broom closet tomb.
Truth-Is dropping a news bomb:
    "Ayo, this just in:
    The next Risin' Barz contest—
    the latest flash event
    hosted by the Legendary King Heavy—
    is gonna go down tonight, y'all!"

Truth's vid cuts to footage of Heavy tearing it up in the 90s.
Mel perks up, focuses on her phone, Heavy her hero.
Truth-Is offers intimate narration, all like:
    "I heard a rumor Heavy's got it so on-lock,
    he turned down distribution deals with Aftermath
    and Def Jam just 'cuz he can. Doesn't need 'em.
    And now the mogul's returning to the spot
    where he made his brand in the M.I.A.: Club Valdemar.
    Yah, the one with the rep for being haunted—
    Emcees betta hurry if they wanna catch a royal blessing.
    The star-maker's gonna find his next supernova
    on our watch, so aspiring rhymers start stressing."
Life-changing break ready for the taking. Gotta be fate
swooping in right before the poison-mimosa dam breaks.

Mima peeks in—her co-worker, who also happens to be mom,
aka Angel Z, perpetually heartbroken monogamist serial.
    "Break's over, Melody," she says.

So formal.
Forever scent of jasmine lotion.
Mel pockets her phone, Pretty-Dope, aspiring emcee
plotting on how to compete in the show.
Strides away from the mirror of soap graffiti.
Comes back, washes it off.
One day, she'll be boss.
But first, she's gotta conjure funds.
Clock ticking and speeding up.

⧫

Opportunity awaits—if she can get her way.   140
Mel scrubs a window, determined to escape,
define a new fate. *Spray, spray.*
Mima going on from the hotel room's bathroom,
pushing back on Mel's request:
  "You need to be thinking about going back to
  school, getting a tech degree or something—"
    "To drown in debt with no floaties?
    Nah, I got dreams—"
"Dreams are for sleep. You're sleepwalking.
Gonna walk out in traffic and get yourself killed.   150
Best worry about paying bills."
    "I just need a chance, Mima."
"We need that money."
    "Lauryn needed Wyclef Jean to put her on—"
"Save it."
    "Lil Kim needed Biggie—"
"I said, save it."
      "Hear me out. Tupac needed Digital
      Underground; D'Angelo needed…

I don't know—"
"Girl, I said—"
        "Everyone's gotta get a shot.
        C'mon,
        you love Tupac."
"He sure was fine. D'Angelo too.
Heard he got fat, though,
lost that sexy six-pack, so…
Nena, you trapped in the 90s,
barely born. Best pay attention
to the present."
Mel's drawn to the past—no beef with the current,
nothing to squash—just pulled by the roots.
Like absolute proof. Veracity.
Voraciously educated by search engines.
Sponsored by Google, Wiki, and YouTube.
Project Guggenheim feeding her the clues
to find and climb the Sequoia of Knowledge.
Soundtracked by hip-hop, trip hop, jazz, folk, funk,
and fusion, rock, and rock 'n' roll, soul, and neo soul, dub,
grunge, alternative, world music, and classical.
Making endless logs of favorites and observations, and mix-
        tapes and playlists.
Finding parallels between the discographies of OutKast and
        The Beatles.
Tracklists ranging, and stretching, like train tracks across time
        and space.
Absorbing fragments of art in her head before bed…
Van Gogh, Japanese prints—Celia Cruz, Frida Kahlo,
pollinating her subconscious.
Meanwhile, Mima talking about: *You can afford college.*

And Mel trying to convey:
Chica, I wouldn't touch it with a 10-foot scholarship—
I wanna be a star. Any other path, rather be departed.
Time's the most important thing.
Schools not teaching it, or emotional intelligence, or
    money management,
or mindful awareness.
Consciousness, of no consequence.
Mel's skeptical of tools measurable via Scantrons scribbled with
    #2s.   200
Mima still going on:
    "Don't change the subject.
    Bottom line—"
        "Mima, I'm doin' this for us.
        So we can bust free of all…"
Cleans up a used condom on the carpet:
        "…this."
Rubber-gloving tourists' DNA gonna leave her DOA
one day, just wait—even if genes say we're 99% the same—
point she's trying to make.   210
Her mom scrubbing the tub, on her knees.
Exactly the fate Mel's aiming to flee.
Mima like:
    "Said, don't change the subject.
    You wanna blow your paycheck
    on a rap contest."
        "At least I ain't blowin'—
        oops, wrong choice of words."
Hitting Mima low, Mel knows.
    "Girl, I'm 'bout to slap you upside the head,   220
    what that smart mouth deserves."

"I'm just sayin' this contest gonna be hot lit."
But she's struck the beast, sparked the fuse;
Mima erupting—unleashed—as she's prone to do,
zero-to-sixty over something iffy.
No one talking Mima down when
Cubana's riled richly. Exploding
from the hotel room's bathroom,
always able to put the fear of doom from Oshun
—or other Afro-Cuban gods—   230
in Mel—Orishas, specifically.
    "All that music,
    all that history,
    all that trivia you got
    memorized,
    all you done heard, done seen, what
    that shady biz done to folks, even
    ones who done made it. Straight
    poison. Fulla vultures,
    fleas, fakes, cannibal rats   240
    chasing scraps.
    You want *that* to love you?"
Mel squeezes the dirty rag
into a bucket. *Fuck it.*
But how's she gonna get this cash?
Can't back down so fast; this chance could be her last.
Done seen what the other road holds—*"keep your head low,"*
"play your role"—instructions that failed Rosa, her day-one
    BFF; struck down
in her prom gown by a stray bullet on her way home.   250
Straight A's couldn't save her.
Mel cradled her, lied encouraging words—helpless,

31

witnessing Rosa's desires expire like fireflies snowing upward.

Mima winces pain from her hip—grimaces—
been happening since before the diagnosis, whenever she
    moves too quick.
Mel tries to help her sit, but the Cubana rejects the chair,
still pissed. Her bones sick. Cold shit. No way to ease her
    disease, terminal.
No coverage to change her condition, no spirit gifts to balm it.
Sometimes Mel wants to vomit and bomb it all—*the world*—
    for what it's doing to Mima.
Sore subject. Hopping off tip. Can't tell what the future holds.
    Gotta hold life tight,
and live like you might not make it back to the abode tonight.
So, Mel stands her ground, bracing for a slap,
wishing she had a dad to ask—
says to her mom, who gave her the human condition:
    "Just tell your cuddy-buddy boss
    I want my money."

❧

The sting, deeper than her skin—
Mima's palm reverberating through Mel's cheek,
even three hours later, cratering her prayers.
Desperate, Mel washes dishes, working up a sweat.
Maid's blouse hanging on a peg, tank-top soaking wet.
Her arms steeped in oil and water.
SPLASH. SCRUB. STACK.
SPLASH. SCRUB. STACK.
Pondering her next steps:
Gotta take her issues past the middle-mom and bad puns.

Finish the shift and demand the gruyère from Greg the Boss.
If dude refuses, grab something expensive and dash.
What's the cost of making it?
Which sins does she gotta check off the list to experience bliss?
Her ex-first love, who broke her bust—Thou Who Shall
     Remain Nameless—
said it was *"hopeless"*—*"…let it go, know your role"*—
didn't even believe in her—Gemini treated her like shit.
Now, Mel's never gonna settle again.
SPLASH. SCRUB. STACK.   290
SPLASH. SCRUB. STACK.
Staccato strut of ceramics.
Blues invoking her spiritual muse.
Mel freestyling to herself like she's become used to:
    "H2O flows
    But the dough never grows
    Or even shows
    Much less goes
    In my pockets
    What I gotta do to stock it?   300
    Hungry, with these empty pockets"
SPLASH. SCRUB. STACK.
SPLASH. SCRUB. STACK.
    "Grungy goddess
    Why be modest?"
SPLASH. SCRUB. STACK.
SPLASH. SCRUB. STACK.
    "Washing other folks' dishes
    Left out of recognitions
    In the doldrum ditches…   310
    Tryin' to live on wishes—"

"You go, girl."
Interrupted by Greg the Boss.

Mel spins, exposed.
Finds him closer than he sounded; she notices, you know this.
His Acapulco shirt soaking in her sweat by osmosis. Bogus.
        "Bravo. What a show."
She grabs her blouse from the peg.
Buttoning. Eyes on the clock.
    "There's the whistle.
    Now about that bank note for
    services rendered—"
Greg closes shut the door, CLICK.
Shit—Mel glances around: knives, pans, bone gristle.
Greg meets her eyes, waves cash, whistles. Offers
it to her. She snatches it, counting.
    "Where's the rest?"
        "Coming."
Stares at her
chest. Squarely.
She dashes for the door. *Fuck this stress.*
He slows her. Offers more dough. Pickled in cologne.
        "With a Christmas bonus."
    "Christmas comin' early."
Santa Claus oozing suspicious cause. *Hint, hint.*
Looking for someone to jiggle jingle-bell balls. Kris Kringle,
the horn-dog boss who happens to be splacking and shacka-
    lacking mom.
Jeez, what a jizz, all that jazz. He says:
        "I don't know much about music,
        but you sound like what I think it

should sound like, you know?"

Mel can't help but soften,
like: *You really think so?*
    "C'mon, you don't gotta front."
Greg swearing, like: *No stunt.*
        "No fronting."
Mel still not buying it,
but something in her wanting to purchase it nonetheless.
    "Pinky swear and hope to die and fry?"
        "I think you can go places
        with this music thing. Your
        momma said you wanna enter
        some battle or go up for some gig.
        And if this helps you win,
        won't be the worst thing.
        You dig?"
Disarmed,
she sees him take out a little more green.
        "No one makes it alone. Ain't that widely known?"
He offers her the thin stack…
        "We all need someone to believe in us,
        push the right buttons, lend a helping hand,
        just gotta let it be."
She takes it, hesitant but flattered.
Then he reaches for her top—
Fuck.

She processes options: *Report him to who—or is it whom?*
Probably get accused of stealing from tourists, or something,
    herself instead.

Local police gonna pick Greg—or any other prick—over a girl.
Familiar pattern. Not staggering. Nothing Earth-shattering.
Gather the evidence to scatter it. What does it matter then?
No surprise. Mel just hoped it wouldn't come to this.
Knows all too well this form of silent carousel—
foul, musky smell, watching his smile swell.
A cell. Hell. But then she thinks: *What the hell—
gotta have enough dough to escape this jail.
Ain't no Salvation comin' in the mail.*
Apparent cost of rising up the ladder.   380
And so, Mel lets it slip,
happen, boundaries snapping—
Catches her reflection in a rack of Ginsu knives—sick,
can't even look
as the next button
unhooks—
CLICK.

Track 3

Valdemar

AFTER OVER NINETY-FIVE miles on 95 South, a
Greyhound leaves Mel
  with a WHOOSH on a mean street in the rain, soul-
  dirtied, stained,
skin feeling foreign, wondering: does doing what she did take
  away from who she is?
Tarnish her as Dolly Parton warned in an interview Mel
  once saw?
Does she even wanna know the truth? Pimped butterflies in
  her stomach,
she wants to puke. Bad taste what her mood is. A Brutus to
  herself what the scoop is.
Still, what was she supposed to do?
And does each rung of the ladder host a sprung dude?
Wishing the rain will exorcise the Judas in her brain—
wash her heart, soul, and mind clean.

Pipe dream. *Drip, drop, plop* at the bus stop.
Spiteful humidity slapping her hoodie.
Chances are the agua won't cease.
Holding herself under a streetlamp's orange sodium-vapor glow
    in the epicenter
of nowhere. Beat-up buildings, stray cats, and broken glass.
    Distant sirens howl
on the soundtrack.
And a random duck's walking around?
Artifacts on the wrong side of the train paths.
Mel kicks away a syringe, crosses herself—
less faith, more superstition. Trying not to listen
to a badgering feeling. Praying to an Afro-Cuban god,
just in case, saying:
    "21-Faced Trickster Orisha called Eleguá,
    Deity of Roads, taking on the personage of a kid on
        a corner,
    whom Catholics call El Niño de Atocha,
    open up this path, and close the bad—
    bless me with the essential life force of àṣẹ:
    the power to effect change—help me
    win, so I never have to go back to live in Central Florida
    and please watch my back."
Is that some dude smoking crack around the corner?
Can't bother 'bout that. Gotta figure out where the action's at.
    "How you holdin' up, Miles?"
Checking on her tiny goldfish, who swims in a 24-ounce water
    bottle from Zephyrhills
holstered to her backpack.
Her Adidas tap the wet sidewalk, nervous.
Can't tell for sure if it's the torrent or the nerve sweat making
    her clothes wet.

At least she's out of her maid fatigues; in torn and rolled-up
    retro Guess jeans,
piercings back in—one nostril sporting a star stud, on the
    other side, a nose cuff,
cubic zirconia butterfly charm, a mic between wings for
    the larvae.
King Heavy-halter top under sleeveless hoodie, pink like her
    shell-top kicks.
Straight outta beats by Rick Rubin. No other rings, chains, or
    bling at all—can't afford a thing.
Intimidated in this land of Rick Ross and Trick Daddy. She
    wraps the cord around her headphones, no Bluetooth (that
    old), unhooks her retro Walkman, goes to tuck it away but
—the contents—
of her backpack spill out—
        "Fuck a shit—"

Drops seven cassettes,
three library paperbacks: Collected Poems by Hughes, Poe,
    Angelou,
and one lyric book
to the ground. Horrible sound.
Scrambles to refill the bag. Feeling the stacking pressures of
    little catastrophes.

Then she hears the precious sound of BASS BOOMING across
    the street…
        "Could that be it?"
She's finally arrived.
In the land of Gloria Estefan, Miami Sound Machine;
    mi tierra,

Mel's thinking, hearing congas, feeling a cosmic link.
Don Francisco from Sábado Gigante's in the vicinity.
Watermelon Man percussionist Mongo Santamaría's buried   80
    near here.
Mel cautiously maneuvers between haggard palms and fronds,
    and finds:

Jagged clouds pounding down on an isolated theater
—free-standing, multi-storied—
boxed in by a rusty fence. Deco Gothic. Retro neon pink
"**CLUB VALDEMAR**" sign
above the door; another loose on the roof,
coloring the place, from the box office ticket booth base to
    the tower   90
touching the moon, an eerie glow. Otherworldly, like so: rain-
    drops neon-haloed.
Humidity gravitational. Patrons wrapped around the spot in
    a knot.
Feeding off the energy like a black hole, massive.
Mel's read all about it, story episodic:
informed by BuzzFeed and Wikipedia on the topic:
A hotel ship capsized and clogged the harbor
to Miami, the Magic City, back in the Roaring 1920s
land boom bloom—until a hurricane came   100
and broomed it all away.
Then Club Valdemar was built,
the name a topical joke. Cousin of the Coconut
    Grove Playhouse,
Jackie Gleason Theater, and Les Violins Supper Club.
Marquee lights and gold leaf inside.
Now, the tropical joint's preservation has been pummeled

by politics and business—bull market for
    luxury condominiums.
That's why the HUM of generators under the
    BOOMING BASS
shows this show's happening outside the system. Just listen.
Calling her to come, as if alive,
Poe's House of Usher-like.
Blackened-out windows, the black eyes.
Edifice, a face shrouded-like; can just make out the entrance:
a lion's mouth—ticket booth like a gapped tooth.
Summoning this girl.
The thrust vertical, tower stretching to vertigo. Ornate former
    cabaret, not playing.
Symmetrical
Art Deco style. Facade terra-cotta, cast stone. Erected, clad
    with Gothic-style tracery.
Marquee flickering askew typewriter keys. Spooky. Empty
    traces where the rest would be.
History sprinkled with mystery, wrapped in artificial mist.
Aura growing more aphrodisiac-kissed.
Mel floating toward it,
since the moment she spotted the establishment,
as if drawn hypnotically. Miles the goldfish swimming
in the bottle as Mel bypasses an outer fence that rocks
a "**CONDEMNED: PROCEED AT YOUR OWN RISK**" sign like cor-
    roded bling.
Steps around puddles deep as ditches, signs of climate change
    far from subtle.
Groups huddled like cool kids avoiding school until the
    bell rings.

Mel solo—no poles for her to split alone, hopes her luck isn't
     in decline as she navigates
an incline. Neon reflecting on the street, off the wet concrete.   140
     Hues under her feet as she steps: purples, blues, and pinks.
     Smell of hot rain, skunk weed, vapes, and nicotine.
Emcees and attendees congregating under palm tree canopies.
Finally, a chance to prove and show.
Been catching the Holy Ghost over poetry and prose since she
     was barely five or six-years old.
Rapper seeking delights atop Sugarhill, Rapture like Debbie
     Harry fronting Blondie
in a Fab Five Freddie clip.
Mel GarageBanded a trove of demos, hoping for exposure. But   150
one's treasure is another's garbage.
Mixtapes low on clicks, so she's grown desperate,
not so sure anymore, more unsure. Hard to crack the system
     when you're lost
in a YouTube algorithm.
Pleading: *Please, please listen to my demo*, like the EPMD song,
Please, Please, like the Beatles begging Decca before signing
     with Capitol.
Just wants people to believe she's good.
Please, please 'cuz it's all she's got to ask, and a long road to go,   160
hoping a Midas will take her hand, hoping even more
     it's Heavy,
her number one, her kindred soul.
(Her day one, Rosa, always used to be encouraging, say,
     "Of course!")
The king's legendary verses making both feel less alone. Now
     Mel's reaching out to

ring on the same tone. Either win—or *blow* like the wind, and
    her mom, and what she did
herself earlier on, and go home.   170
Mel slows
at a circle of devotees,
entranced by the siren song
of another emcee, a Master of Ceremonies:
as seen on YouTube, as heard on SoundCloud,
flamboyant and fiery Kandela Del Fuego with the thick red
    streak in her hair;
old by Mel's standards, must be 30 or so, but still tearing
    shit down;
covered with piercings and things, owning the assemblage.   180
Cute Cuba-Rican alpha diva in an Aladdin-pants jumpsuit.
Acting like she just don't care and her shit don't stink.
Contralto's voice deeper than Mel's alto on the register:
    "Kandela reppin' for the homies rockin' DADE Wear
    And fades from Kulayed, so wake up the nightmare
    Tell 'em I'm here, bringin' the fear
    Y'all heard it here
    Jekyll & Hyde betta hide, and steer clear
    I dropped the Cyclops and his pop!
    Fight the power, fuck the police and the cops!   190
    What y'all fuckers got?!"
Sticks out a tongue ring, stud of a grinning skull, wagging
it all: *"Ahhh!!!»*
Mel bewitched. Kandela, the kool witch, finishing with:
    "So y'all better cheer
    Take it—"
Only now does Mel realize she's in a cypher,
encircled by emcees freestyling—

Kandela Del Fuego bearing down on her, intense
as La Lupe performing Latin soul in 1960s New York, like: 200
    "Go head, girl. Lay it down, let it go."
Other emcees, like:
    "Or turn around!"
        "And bend down!"
            "And do it now, hoe!"
Great (Jill) Scott!
All of the following goes through her cranium in an instant:
Wonderland Alice in the war zone—here it is—even if it's in an
    unofficial warmup,
a prelude to what you've been training for, like Great Apollo Creed   210
toking Golden Age hip-hop.
Inhaling Tribe, De La, Bizarre Rides II the Pharcyde—
proverbial pipe packed, intoxicating you on vibes, auditory
    cortex high
outta sight, transcending time, like hearing them live.
Epic catalogue—just from that era alone.
Inhibitions inebriated uninhibited, inspiring you to
    break boundaries
like Public Enemy, Run-DMC, Beasties, Biggie, OutKast, Goodie
    Mo-B,   220
Fugees, Badu, Tupac, Wu-Tang, Busta, Bootcamp
Clique, Eric B. & Rakim, Slick Rick, Jeru, Redman, Big Daddy
    Kane, Funkdoobiest,
Organized Noize, Organized Konfusion;
soothe the soul like the Roots; spark a protest like the Coup;
rise iconic like Jay, Nas, Common and Snoop;
pure as parties on Sedgwick, where hip-hop was born—
brilliant as KRS: Knowledge Reign Supreme Over
    Nearly Everyone;

MF DOOM on MM FOOD—mm good, serve it up   230
nimble as Supernatural the Freestyle King; wise as Big Rube,
Rah Digga, Roxanne, Digable Planets, Gangsta Boo, Rock & Smooth,
Queen Latifah, Missy Elliot, Mary J., J5, Bahamahdia,
Salt-N-Pepa—BEP, Blackalicious, Delicious Vinyl,
    Jazzyfatnastees—
under the influence of so many influences, instigating
your love of busting flows, addiction jonesing for a fix to binge,
    increasing by the moment—
MC Lyte, MC Shan, MC Ren, Eminem,
Slum Vill, Dr. Dre, NWA, Masta Ace, Scarface, Hieroglyphics,   240
Alkaholiks (aka Tha Likwit)—euphoric euphoria in Stankonia,
    craving underground cred
like Company Flow, Guru and Primo, Cypress Hill,
    Swollen Members,
Kweli and Mos—music beating in your soul. That's the scenario.
Caged bird ready to exhale, ready to sing, ready to flow—
                until it don't.

Melody freezes. Speechless.
Withdraws her deposit,
backs away without busting,   250
or dropping,
or laying down
a flow.
Nowhere near, or close, to Sly Stone—or Sly Stallone
going toe-to-toe with the great Apollo.
      "My bad… gotta go."

Total fail. Colossal choke.
What a joke.

Why's she even want this life for?
Oh, right:
Just the only dream she's ever known.
Stage fright always part of her ride, toll for the road
when it doesn't totally slow her roll.

They jeer, leer, move on without her.
Kandela all like:
> *"Poor girl can't show and prove*
> *But I can flow the truth*
> *She can go, forget the emcee booth,*
> *Give up - it's no use"*

Mel hears them, keeps going.
Embarrassed,
can't have any more of that if Eleguá's gonna open up a path.
Bitching about herself to Miles:
> "What kind of wack-ass shit was that?"
Questions the race. Questions race.
Questions herself, of mixed race;
is her love of hot music and the hop,
her Cuban heritage, and heartbeat in clave enough—
or is her hambone an appropriation? Cultural diffu-
sion confusion.
Could she be like that blonde, candy emcee in that
indie movie—
decent flow, considered a thief and a joke?
What'll happen when she's past 40, older than John Lennon
and Poe ever were?
Craving Fame like Irene Cara, who was, like, 18 when she
made it.

Oh, Mel, what a failure. Halloween-scary.
Can't even shop for a tat; how sad is that?

290

Meekly, she navigates through the outside throng,
bumped and pushed around, squeezing toward
the VIBRANT SOUND, finds two lines:
one marked "SPECTATORS" (full of haters)
the other "COMBATANTS" (full of wackness)
or so she hopes,
carrying herself like *a dope*
instead of just being Dope.
Does she have the corazón to cope, thrive, survive?
Questions out on Pretty-Dope. Survey
says: *Don't hold your breath.*

300

Her phone vibrates. Two texts
from Mima, surprisingly not bat-shit:
    ["don't waste ur life"]
    ["come home"]
Tempting—till another text hits her phone,
from Greg:
    ["Make that sweet mouth famous"]
Mel gives her phone screen the finger. Shuts it off.
Determined to stir up a fuss, cause chaos, burn some shit up.

310

✍

At the once-lush entrance under the flickering marquee,
paper rips, rustles as Mel receives a signup sheet.
In front of a box office girl, who looks put-upon
popping gum at the gate to the kingdom.
BASS LOUD enough Mel can feel the low end in her chest,

her bosom beating to the beat even out on the street,
dirty rain washes weathered marble tiles under her sneaks.

Mel fills the torn form quick:
• *Name:* BONITA DOPENESS
aka PRETTY-DOPE
• *Over 21?* Yes.
Leaves the Home blank, empty address.
Signs the Talent Release—offers back the sheet.
Box Office Girl takes her sweet time to review it
in hoop earrings, paid on someone else's dime.
Forcing Mel and the rest to wait for fate to kick in.
Mel sees the proprietors against a wall, conferring
out of the storm. She read about them in a piece
about the battle over the theater, renovation versus demolition.
Article even featured a picture.
Mom-and-pop Cuban couple, escapees of the Revolution.
And their muscular sons in Nike suits. Keeping the
bathrooms and lights running until the implosion.
Observing the snaking drove like chaperones.
Heavy probably paid them off to book the place
under the radar, since shows ain't condoned.
So clever, Mel thinks, then wonders
what it's like to have a home with a dad and bros.
Box Office girl, popping gum, sayin':
        "Entry fee's three bills. Cash or crypto."
Mel like:
                "Wow, three-hundred dollars?!"
Gum popping to respond:
        "No, cents.
        We running a charity."

Checks the form…
    "Pretty… Dope."
        "It was two earlier."
    "That was the early-bird.
    You missed the worm."   350
Box Office Girl not budging,
call her Notorious B.O.G.
Mel digs through her bag,
pulls cash from the worn Poe
paperback. Some guy's voice says:
                "Pretty-dope book."
A 20-something dude
coming through all smooth. Handsome
B-boy sporting that prep-school style,
light cardigan and Clarks, all Tyler-The-Creator-on-a-Sunday.   360
Unbaked: capillaries white, eyes straight.
Slick kicks; could kick it with a dude like this—
if she wasn't all about the business.
Hope he slips into her DMs down the line some time.
Walkie earpiece. Like the dude's got somewhere to be
but stopped real quick to see who she be.
He adjusts a box of tees in his arms,
rocks a tight do; did she mention nice shoes?
Smells good too. He points at her paperback:
                "You got a new single   370
                    if you put some drums and bass
                    under The Bells; that'd be fresh as hell."
She counts cash, coming up short, too fucked
for small talk—makes some anyway:
                "Maybe The Bells could be the B-side.
                    But the A-side banger would, for sure, be

The Raven."
          "Seems too obvious."
Mel looks back at him. Eyes sublime. Briefly distracted
from the issue at hand. Handsome B-boy, asking Mel:
          "You here to compete?"
    "Jesus, Spur,
    what the fuck?"
B.O.G. exasperated. Saying shit like:
    "Yo, Book Club,
    you gonna pay to play
    or what?
          "Right, my bad.
          About that price tag—"
    "Gotta move this line.
    You outta time."
Rest of the line waiting, debating whether to call out Spur—
none of it helping her. Time to pay up.
Mel reaches into her top.
Withdraws
all the money she's got
left. Rolls up
the random bills. Hands over the cash.
Gambler going all-in.
Spending more than a little to make more than a little.
Taking to heart wisdom
Dave from De La Soul said
on the LP before *Bionix*.
Mel starts to move ahead—
    "Hold up."
B.O.G. counts bills while Mel sweats…
Stops.

"Twenty-one short."
Mel fumbling for a recovery:
        "Lucky digits.
        Story 'bout how you
        gave me a chance
        and I went and won
        gonna be Hiroshima, yo,
        ya know, like the bomb."
B.O.G. hands it back, like:
    "Next!"
When Spur's like:
        "I got you."
Adjusts the box he's holding, takes out cash.
B.O.G. frowns. Mel's first instinct is to stop it
from going down. Tired and sick of going
down. On the ladder, another dude sprung?
        "What's that buy?"
            "Charitable donation."
        "For what cause?"
            "Edgar Allan Poe Fellowship
            of the Arts.
            Take it now—or Nevermore."
Their eyes lock. He smiles at her.
B.O.G. jealous now for sure.
    "Ain't gonna ask again. Next!"
Mel glances at the judging eyes
in line behind her.
Pulls her hand back, allows Spur to pay.
He gets a message in his earpiece,
muffled to her hearing. Listens, then:
        "Shit, tell H I'll be right there."

410

420

430

Mel's eyes zoom in on the Heavy tee
beneath Spur's cardigan. Don't tell her the dude knows 440
Da One Who Only Fucks Wit Da Best,
(as King Heavy, about himself, says).
          "You know His Highness?
          King H? Bettino White?
          Your Pure Majesty?"
So many aliases, but Mel can keep them straight.
Spur doesn't deny the connection, but he muzzles the volume
on the muffled message coming through the earpiece,
like it's not the most amazing occupation.
                    "Yeah, and I gotta go 450
                    put out another fire."
Chemicals and context fueling desire.
                    "See you backstage,
                    Poe-ette," he says.
At the threshold to the eerie venue with a presence,
leaving her contemplating the entrance that's a little wet,
     Spur-of-the-Moment—
his full name, as she would later learn—rushes away to save
     another day.
Interesting dude. And part of the king's crew— 460
might come in handy if Mel tells another joke
when the lights get Red Hot Chili Peppers scorched, and she's
     supposed to perform;
thinking all this as a purple band is wrapped ouch-tight
     around her wrist.
Might as well be a noose for her larynx.
Officially all-in. *This is it.* Broke, no going back, can't afford to
     quit or choke.

Track 4

Rat Pack Exhales

MEL CROSSES THE threshold
into the rundown Deco lobby.
Excited. Ready to ignite shit.
Expectations high in the blacklight,
ultraviolet. Mezzanine. Vestibule.
So off the chain. Too fucking cool.
Bar, concessions, auditorium up ahead.
Past merchandise stands, Heavy-themed:
tees, posters, candles, vinyl LPs—gotta win
herself some of these, get comped free martinis.
Especially in the place
where the legend was crowned, where Heavy became King.
Mel amazed, in a haze, at the hist she's stepping in.

Her Adidas

stepping over once-gleaming Sienna marble floors,
moving past rusted metal finishes,
worn Moroccan marble walls.
Once a place of decadence,
club ain't seen much action since.
Exposed wiring
where chrome sconces would've been—outlines
of their geometric trims.
Back in the day, marble would've reflected
light like slick liquid, streaming
just right. What a sight that must've been,
how hot-lit those nights would've seemed
—whether pre-Depression,
postwar boom, or Y2K—
flappers, Rat Packers and rappers
would've exited after—excited, giggling,
into the dawn light.
What a life!
Now all that's left is ancient nicotine essence,
unfiltered tar smoked into crumbling walls.
Sinatra, Rat Pack exhales.
Kinda sad, rats now stuck living
in the structure's entrails.

She crosses to the club floor, and enters
another world:
Bass thumping. Smoke machines humming.
Flashing multicolored lights splashing in her view
as she surveys the venue—awestruck at the Cinerama.
The attendees secreting juices, like sofrito ingredients
in a Spanish-grotto-style auditorium,

wrapped in alabaster plaster, 20s Americana.
Buying into the majesty,
etching herself into a wall like Banksy,
Mel passes a strange brew of Neo-Deco-Gothic graffiti—
characters, tags and pieces—(EKA Crew repping
    the district)—
Poe meets Tamara de Lempicka,
macabre stories and bold, polished portraits.
Immersive, occult, colors glowing like Cosmos,
dazzling in the dark. Party over here, the sure shot.
As if wandering through a mural of a graveyard
on the grounds of an old mansion—creepy,
cold, drafty, but the guests are hot.
Clothes submerged in liquid salt.
Her eyes a camera, recording it all:
The ceiling resembling a sunburst—
oval dome gilded and tiled with mirrors,
refracting black lights, encircled with sirens and devils.
Place on another level. She's never
seen anything like it in person.

Mel's eye-aperture tightens focus.
Her lens set on the stage coiled behind faded red curtains
as a DJ spins titan vinyl in front of the drapery,
warming up the crowd below the crystal drop chandelier
with speakers bathed in incandescence.
Candelabras blooming like calendulas
before the rap opera tournament
even starts. But can she endure, when it does,
huh? Mel stares up—still awed—gets pushed aside
by Kandela Del Fuego, looming larger than in the cypher,

disdain-pity-mixed gaze easy to decipher:
    "Lights on, little girl."
Take a tickle to kindle Kandela herself as she and her crew
    run roughshod
past Mel, seemingly the only one without a squad,
a green blueberry on an island.
She tugs at the purple band wrapped around her wrist,
trying to loosen it. Interrupted by the crowd,
crush pushing, amassed in all directions, spinning her
to and fro in the gumbo—dizzying.
Adidas stepped on by high heels and designer cleats.
Drinks spilled. *Oh, hey, there's another bar—yo, watch out for*
    the kicks!
Floor sticky. Mel's head spinning, turning. Feeling low—
slow—lost in the jungle. Not welcome.
Guns in waistbands, but no roses, appetite for destruction.
Prolonged civil war inside and outside her,
like La Violencia with Colombia, where her absentee father's
    family's from.
All these thoughts on Mel's mind
    as it melds with Club Valdemar.
Same time, Mel senses she's being watched.
Looks up, her glance grazes
the mezzanine—passing
shuttered private boxes
as a neon beam hits one—
witnesses something through the slats:
a
spectator
specter
slipping

into shadows.

Mel looks again.
That was no bathroom mirror vision,
no graffiti from her imagination.
Spirit of the premises. Some sort of presence. Spectral presets.   110
Valdemar's haunted, Mel can tell—feel it
under the lobby's vaunted vaulted ceiling—feel it
like the skin on her back and arms crawling—feel it
like the sweat she's leaking from her forehead, crotch,
     and cleavage.
Mel's always seen the dead, like:
her old Abuelita at the foot of the bed;
and her day one, Rosa, as Mel shed her bloody prom dress;
and once a Cuban guajiro laborer
under a palm tree with one leg,   120
stoic, standing under the leaves,
steady as a breeze with no malicious intent.
But something about this feels different instead,
as if it's a night in Hell Mel's about to spend.
Already having one of those hard grey days like Adele.

Unnerved, Mel shakes it off. *Probably just nerves.*
She checks the time. Anxious as ever.
Telling herself: *Maybe it's a good omen,*
maybe it's a guardian angel.

❧

Panicking, Mel cold-washes her face   130
in the ladies' room with rusted faucets.

Rundown like the rest of the place—out of time and space.
    And spacious.
All symmetrical marble, dark green, a toilet-encrusted emerald.
Plastered posters from past eras, clippings. Collages faded
from other ages, sepia-colored newspaper/magazine pages.
Chipped paint. Pastels and extreme shapes, mid-20th Century
pomp and paraphernalia.
What the fuck am I doing here?
In her reflection, more imagination graffiti:
an "L" at the top,
then more letters circle her face,
spelling out "LOSER."
Xeroxed. Multiple instances fill the mirror.
Then Mel gets startled by a clique of vixens coming in
laughing. She moves from the mirror. *Get yourself
together.* Goes into a stall to… stall.
She sets a timer on her phone. Pops
into her retro Walkman a cassette.
Trying to go to her quiet location. Eyeing the timer.
But it's not quite right. Hear girls coming and going,
laughing, joking, shouting, sipping tea (gossiping)—
    who knows.
Mel digs through her backpack as Miles stirs
in the holstered bottle. *Where the fuck is it?*
She pulls out:
Seven cassettes. Three paperbacks. Zero lyric books.
Thinks back to the contents of her backpack spilling
out in the rain.
Fuck.
Mel's first instinct:
Go after it.

But she sees the timer bleeding seconds.
Not enough to go around.
     "Fuck a shit!"
Voices respond:
          "What's up in there, girl?"
               "You okay, Mami?"
                    "Drama going down everywhere
                    in this theater, telling y'all!"
     "Anybody seen a lyric book? Has a Heavy
     sticker on the front. And—"
          "Lyric book?"
               "Why doesn't she just keep the rhymes
               on her phone?"
                    "Or go off the top of the dome?"
Not what Mel needed to hear.
     "Forget it."
          "Better for the environment, too."
     "Forget it."
               "Yo, you gonna tie everything back
               to that environmental trip tonight, Cassandra?"
                    "I'm saying, though, right?"
     "Consequence of the truth.
     Lyric books are dead trees."
     "Forget it, please."
          "Such a downer, though."
     "Here, have an upper."
          "Why, yes, don't mind if I do."
               "So, why doesn't she just keep the rhymes
               on her phone? That Q been A'ed?"
These people of no use.
     "Fuckin' forget it! Seriously."

170

180

190

"Alright, Dorothy. You brought it up."
"Good luck."
"So, like I was saying about
extreme climate change..."
House lights start flashing
as Mel's alarm buzzes.

Show time.
Mel rushes back late to the auditorium,
an arrow to a target, seeking bullseye—
launched by a quivering archer.

Crowd on her peripheral. Stomach in a knot.
Closing in on the proscenium thrust.
Green room without enough room
for all the emcees trying to kickstart legacies,
so there's a sea of them corralled in a bullpen
at the base of the orchestra pit lining the stage.
Her purple wristband checked
before she's allowed to participate.
Imposter syndrome threatening insurrection
in her brain—unsure how to beat this gang,
who look so much more prepared for this contest.

Curtains part, reveal Heavy,
specs of gray in his fade, crossing the stage to cheers at
     first sight.
The king clad in a purple-silk guayabera,
evoking a macho regal riff on the spirit of gua-
     jira Guantanamera.
Matching suede shoes. Black bowler

with signature purple bow, gold and white-gold crown
adorned with rubies and amethysts, the same min-
    eral combination
as his Versace shades. Violet-tinted lenses, gold and white-
    gold frames
worn by the legend, shining down from the prosce-
    nium heaven.
Mel beholds her idol, stargazing and starstruck, damn near
    close enough to touch.
Crowd out of their seats, stomping their feet,
applause raining down in sheets.
Shedding stardust Heavy brings up the mic, king with his
    scepter. Cigar
in the other hand, rings glinting—rubies, amethysts.
    "Ayo, Miami?!
    Who yo boy?!"
Mel amid the madness as it's unleashed,
fists pumping, screaming, whistling, fans snapping pics,
phone lights igniting the night, Mel's eyes holding tight
on Heavy. Ravenous pit bulls like:
        "HEAVY! HEAVY! HEAVY!"
Mel gazes up in wonder. Studies the king command
    the stage—
his kingdom, throne on a platform—confident in his name,
like K Dot, Anderson .Paak ampersand Pac all wrapped up
    in one.
A boss. A Greco-Roman god: Zeus, Poseidon, Apollo…
even let him fuck your mom.
Heavy like:
    "What I thought."
        "HEAVY! HEAVY! HEAVY!"

"Now I'm 'bout to let y'all know
how shit goes."
        "HEAVY! HEAVY! HEAVY!"
Mel overwhelmed by the tide.
Heavy like:
    "Y'all, there be a lot on the line:
    Ten Gs, a deal with the royal label,
    Raw-Y'all Records, and a chain like the king's.
    Y'all Gs best be ready to shine."

He raises his chain—gold and white-gold and diamonds,
bling featuring **"Raw-Y'all Records"**
and the logo: King Heavy's silhouette with a mic and a crown;
the chain a holy grail to Mel.
Like 3 Tonys, 4 People's Choice and 5 Grammys to her.
An Oscar for Best Song. Emmy, EGOT…
all the above and below:
All the MTV VMAs, BET, and Billboard Awards
bundled into one to her. A golden ticket
to a chocolate factory. So hungry for it. So thirsty—
all right to say it: It means the whole world to her.
A way to save Mima, live for a reason.
So caught up in the awards season, she hasn't heard
what Heavy's said since, words going in one ear,
out the other, not processing.
    "…So, this ain't ya typical tourney.
    You ain't gonna see no entourages
    crowding the stage, acting rowdy.
    Just the emcees going about it."
Behind him, a LARGE SCREEN
displays the contest's banner:

"RI$IN' BARZ"

"Open up them NittyGritty apps."
Without stammer, the crowd around Mel obliges.
The STAGE SCREEN MORPHS
to a graffiti-font LIST of hopefuls.
Mel finds her handle "*Pretty-Dope*"
—Incredible. Beams in her soul.
Heavy, meanwhile, like:
    "We finna start with a qualifyin'.
    Each of y'all gets forty-five ticks
    to bust a freestyle."
Mel sees him looking down at her, waving his scepter:
    "Don't blow it."

She stares into his eyes.
Gotta be good, gotta be great—channel an emcee Kali Uchis,
    rap solid like Rapsody,
in bloom like a Gershwin tune—or was that *in Blue*? Was
    Nirvana *In Bloom*?
Whichever, whatever. Never mind *Nevermind*.
Serve it up: Verbal Molotov. A shock to the chakras.
    Heavy like:
    "After each emcee drops a flow, y'all grade 'em.
    At the end of the round, we finna tally the scores."
Mel gulps, feeling the weight of his stare.
Heavy scans the rest of the faithful, forgetting her:
    "Top eight move onto what we alls
    really wanna see: the battles!"
The coalescence around Mel roars. Heavy calling to action:
    "Emcees, rappers,

like Gang Starr used to say:
'Time to STEP IN THE ARENA!'
Let's do this thang."

The FLOCK ERUPTS.
Heavy drops his microphone
like an old girlfriend, and swaggers to his throne, puffing
    the Cubano.
Mel stares at the discarded mic like it's been dipped in gold.

Track 5

The Live Version

THE BEAT SCRA-SCRATCHES—
DJ-scratched samples:
"Em -
    cees -
        DROP -
           THAT -
             SHIT!"

Wheelz of steel spinning,
808-BEATS BREAKING
out of vinyl grooves
as emcees line up cheered on by their crews.
Meanwhile, solo dolo, Mel steps onstage,
first time in front of an audience this huge,
like a virgin, Madonna at the dawn of her age.

10

Gazing out at the crowd—a sea of phone screens
where she knows lighters used to be, still a cloud of marijuana
	over it;
despite the cannabis, their faces as friendly as a firing squad
	in Hades,
a wrathful god there's no escaping.   20

ROUND ONE, EMCEE PRELIM.
One mic. One line. One light.
A LARGE ELECTRIC CLOCK counts down
the time as Mel observes scribes in line ahead
of her. Experienced in front of a crowd,
same as she's unlearned. Breath control in check.

Not all the contestants good, but the good ones surging.
Mel's concerns emerging—
the competitions' rhymes phat, presences urgent,
performing with the precision   30
of surgeons; Mel's mind wracked
with doubt about how long she'll stick around
if she can't win the crowd
against magicians wielding words like Merlin,
Mel observant as spells are cast,
and wack emcees—along with demons—are cast out.
How she supposed to act now?

Stage Fright and Fear of Failure
rearing their features again. Old enemies.
Monsters. One a fire, blindingly bright;   40
the other a dark void of insignificance and blight.
Hurtling everything they got at her,

making her want to hurl and curl into fetal early.

Worried she's about to fall victim to skills ample;
for example:

- Lil Bone-A-Part, teenaged dread with pop-star style:
  "Burning bubonic chronic
  Slurping gin and tonic on
  Supersonic jets with Jacuzzis
  With jets with girls which is wet
  Bone-A-Part winning bets versus vets
  Getting sweaty Jennys to give floozy neck
  In discotheques - next!"

A few bars and done. Making it seem easy,
even though Mel knows it's not.
The next emcee moving
down the line, SPOTLIGHT
getting closer to her. Beholding:

- Kandela Del Fuego, red-streaked-hair-energy-explosion:
  "Spacey, hazy, so fucking crazy — what's that
  No emcee gonna tame she — got that?
  Chase me, debate me, ain't no playa wanna date me,
  So I tape thee, bring mo' scandal than any Gate, G.
  Peep that. Take it to the Supreme Court like a lady,
  RAT-A-TAT-TAT-TAT with the boom bap
  'Cuz I'm so fucking zany, baby!"

Waves a hand in Mel's vicinity:
  "All these wannabe jits in line are just fucking babies!"

Dissed, confidence shaken once again,

Mel's nonetheless forced to step closer,   70
butterflies buzzing, a swarm—gauging success
through the crowd's contortions,
and the body language
of the triumphant emcees, egos enormous—
social Darwinism, gotta evolve like Gorillaz—or
        involve Gravediggaz.
Mel feeling unsteady, less and less ready. Moving ahead.
        Eyes on:

•   Designer shade-wearing V@$T @ppe@l,
who used to be B@!$ @ppe@l but changed it   80
to M@$$ @ppe@l,
before Nas named his label the same, and it lost
its attractiveness to V@$T.
Mel follows him on SoundCloud and Spotify, and on Insta
        with a Finsta.
V@$T, the angry son of wealthy resources, baritone benefiting
        from a fortune,
bragging on it, pushing wish fulfillment like a dope
        love potion;
be a fool to ignore him.   90
Face tats. Diamond and rose gold chain with his chosen name.
Always remind ya. Grillz to match, name spelled out
        in rhinestone.
V@$T @ppe@l starting his rhyme time with one style, trap-
        ping triplets,
commercial, crowd pleaser:
                *"Flickin' my whip, whip, whip, flickin' my, flickin'
                    my whip, whip, whip*

> *Come git it fo I let it slip, psych, ain't never lettin' go*
> > *of this*   100
> *Whip, whip, whip*
> *Gigolo, got it for a gift, gift, gift, goin' all in, you*
> > *know it"*

Repeating it like a chorus, until he shifts to:
> *"Give it to you how you wanna, with a*
> *Whip, whip, whip, 'bout to flip it on ya,*
> *SKIRT, SKIRT—skidding—"*

Then, he pivots to another style, more old school, battle-ready.
Casting a dismissive glance her way as he snaps:
> *"Listen up, pawns.*   110
> *Bronze bard, surround-sound icon*
> *Goodbye foes, be bygone*
> *All deez bitches on this stage I'm on*
> *Shatter your world like the Doors over*
> *Saigon*
> *Don't know what vibe I'm on?*
> *Give up, go home, put Apocalypse Now on*
> *And strangle yourself with nylon"*

The crowd "OOHS" and "AAHS" with attitude
as he unloads rhymes at emcees in line.   120
Our girl Mel,
just another punching bag and punchline.
But she feels his spite in her spine.

Mel glances at Heavy overseeing the show
from his throne in the orchestra pit. Crowd behind him.
To his right: Sweet Lady Jane—singer, model, actor,
social influencer, and swinger. Her tweets always atwitter.

Crop top and Prada. Coat of arms tat—hearts, wolves,
    blunts—
on her shoulder. Mel's rubbed one out to her before. Who
    hasn't?
To Heavy's left: Nicole Echo-No-Mics, his sister, teased-silver
hair beneath a white fedora, zipper-scar across her cheek,
the result of some unknown, long-ago beef.
Confident confidante in a tight, sensible white dress,
her always-uniform. Patented. Santería beads around her neck,
color combos repping Yoruba gods
(Yemayá, Oshosi, Ogun, Obatalá, and Changó), and a
    silver necklace
with the "Raw-Y'all Records" logo, her holy symbols.
Cell phone and keys always in hand, the fedora-rocking Hand
    of the King;
Mel knows she's the Diddy behind Heavy's Biggie.
So much pressure bubbling in Mel's body—
bumbling, rumbling through her limbs, knees
growing weak—Stage Fright and Fear of Failure fueling her
to perspire hellfire in the seashell footlights' heat
as she's pushed from behind to the mic,
and the spotlight finds her
on beat.

Her turn.

The news like new—BOOM BAP!—Mel thinking:
*Shit! What am I gonna do? What am I gonna rhyme
about? What's my first line?*" Having doubts.

Just wanna rap like Rage, scat like Ella, and paint like
    Artemisia Gentileschi.

The hot light blinding for a moment, then her eyes
    snap open—
darting to the LARGE ELECTRIC CLOCK
TICK-TOCKING down: 160
45, 44, 43…
Don't fuck up. Don't fuck up. Don't fuck up!
She gulps. Mouth dry.
Where she's been stuck in time, thinking
on how she got in the firing line.
Imprisoned in amber. Nightmaring her dream.
The BREAK-BEAT baits her.
She nods, trying to catch a flow.
A KICK and a SNARE waiting
for her to ride them…   170
The BASS flirting kismet and vicious,
like Flea playing for Alanis, and Jaco for Joni.
Hecklers like:
    "Do something, bitch!"
Mind racing with too much to say,
and all of it wrong.
Analysis paralysis. Tongue-tied.
Trying to coach herself, misquoting the real Miles Davis:
Play fewer notes, but the right ones.
Embrace mistakes.   180
There is no wrong note, just the next note you play.
All about the phrasing, but paraphrasing requires phrases,
sounds from the inner depths of the echo chamber,
but the chamber's empty. Betrayed by her body—

et tu?
Again, she feels possessed by a shy stranger.
Or replaced by Jem from the Holograms' alter ego.
Or her courage has been stolen by Carmen San Diego.
Cartoon platoon at high noon. Synergy broken.
Best get some ginger, garlic, and ginseng in your system,   190
    Homer Simpson.
Cinnamon to redeem the sins of man.
Risking being basic.
All that time spilling midnight oil, killing herself to answer
    a call—
What if it's a number that's wrong?
Hiatus waiting.
Crowd against her:
      "Show us your tits!"
Destined to ponder podcasts about Outkast,   200
and make lists comparing Fiona Apples to Blood Oranges;
elbows deep in grease gallows, hotel sink basins, and
    dirty dishes
back in Central Florida, aspirations shipped off to
    arctic storage.
In her peripheral, she sees
Nicole Echo-No-Mics shake her head,
and King Heavy whisper to Sweet Lady Jane, who giggles.
And Mel can glimpse Spur watching in the wings,
the cardigan Casanova seeming concerned.   210
The Box Office Girl appears behind him,
smirking, can almost imagine her words:
      "Still think she's pretty,
       and dope?"
Imagine him thinking: *"Nope."*

Feelings about herself mutual.
Can't even belt out a haiku or a sonnet.
Not in line for honors—syllables and schemes, horrors.
Mel peeps the timepiece. Down
to 10 seconds.
She opens her mouth,
but bupkis
comes
out.
The clock ticks
down…
8,
7,
6…
        "Give up, bitch!"
Choke artist like a slow target.
4-5 seconds, reminding her to say what's on her mind,
like Riri and Paul, if she has the gall. Drawing a blank.
3, 2, 1…
Mel grips her Walkman—at the event horizon—and some-
    thing sparks her.
She jumps on the beat, a real live emcee,
pogoing the drunken meter, reel-to-reel,
as if flowing from an engrained tape,
the essential life force of àṣẹ kicking in:
    "Sick of the sidelines, I gotta get mine
    Shine - divine mind for our times, my advice
    To the gentlemen, ladies, and babies"

King Heavy and Nicole Echo-No-Mics suddenly like:
    Say what?

    "Be an emcee killa
    Before an emcee kill ya
    Do you in for a label
    That can't feel or see ya
    Kill an emcee where it hurts,
    Soft underbelly in the megahertz
    Beat a drum with hooks and bars
    Stab a song in the back, no love"

The clock TICK-TOCKS
to zero. The BEAT STOPS.
And Mel drops
her punctuation
a capella,
tender alto digging deeper, her vocal register crop rising
    with confidence,
Amy Winehouse contralto, commanding
the spotlight—voice and words coming to her
from somewhere elsewhere—
dictated by heavenly maidens
and saintly ladies in waiting
with rude attitudes, Mel goes crude
to compensate for not having a crew,
her eyes locking on Heavy, gaze holding steady,
rhyming right at him, surreal satisfaction:
    "Killa born and reborn a fuckin' orphan
    Dying to pull good from bad
    Like a rabbit from a trap, top hat, or a coffin

Emcee dreams be all a killa ever had
Writing rhymes since I started coughin'
Lying for a rhyme scheme, truth be no later than age five
Now equipped with rhymes for all times
And All Time
—All kinds—
'Cuz it's my time
My time
My time
To design, build and fill shrines"
Everything else fading away, just her and Heavy
left, zoning out bouncer footsteps behind her waiting
to take her away—not doing it yet, so she can't stop
the flow 'til she's done, or they'll make her go.
   "Shoot an intro, cut a line, end a rhythm,
spend a rhyme, hunt a verse, kill a chorus
Put it in a hearse, dispersed, blow up the bridge it's crossing
Crossing signals, drown it in an ocean, mouths open, sing-
     ing along
Crescendo crushing 'em in a song, strangling on a mic cord,
     chord
Change they can't afford, vocal cords collapsing
Shouldn't have gone for that note
But on another…
Repeat, do it again for an outro, terminate the jam, the joint,
     the world
Wanna get something nice for my girls
I'm out, y'all
(All coda, ice cold)
'Cuz I'm an emcee killa,
I'm an emcee killa

75

*ain't none reala - ain't none illa
I'm an emcee killa"*

She releases the mic like a trigger, gets pushed
aside—Heavy still lined up in her sight,
reticle-tight, a spectacle might,
special to see him impacted—bullseye—right in his mind's
    eye, reaction chemical, on his face legible,   310
caught in the spot where it matters by her tentacles (like a kick
    to the...? Nah, psych);
the sound of the legion, crystal clear: they like. Mel surprises
    herself, relishing the moment
like a legend delighting in the spotlight—just as quick,
the magic lantern
leaves her
behind.
The BEAT KICKS IN AGAIN, the next emcee jumps
on the mic.   320

Track 6

Magic Lantern

RUBBING SANTERÍA BEADS
as goosebumps crawl down from her arms to her
spleen to her toes,
Nicole Echo-No-Mics ignores the preliminary show,
staring at the aspiring emcee calling herself Pretty-Dope.
King Heavy, her brother Bettino, leans over, whispers:
 "What the fuck?"
Nicole, honestly in shock, retorts:
 "Warned you about this place,
 H—it's fucking haunted.
 We shouldn't be here."
Throws a frown at their surroundings
from their judges' table throne in the orchestra pit.
Crowd behind them, like on a reality show.
Bettino glaring at her like he's not having it;

always an argument between them when it comes to
religion, spirituality—guilt. Bettino like:
          "King's finna pretend you didn't say that."
             "Save the royal shit with me, Bettino."
          "Then *I'm* finna pretend you didn't say that, Nicole."
             "Facts, bro. Spirits with unfinished business."
          "Spirits gonna suck a four-five Glock off.
          Bleed like errbody else does, ain't no ghosts.
          We finna find out what the fuck, dawg."
Nicole wonders what else her brother needs answered,
when they've just seen what they've seen;
"Emcee Killa" lyrics back from the dead—
silence broken, exposed, out in the open.
Nicole rubs beads down to the string,
zipper-scarred cheek itching, asking Bettino:
             "What do you want me to do?"
Things worse since their head of security died during
    the Recession.
RIP, Sir Skinny, featured on a few tracks, gone too young—
not the only one—really don't wanna think about that.
Save it for deathbed confessions of more stolen rap sessions.
    Point is:
Impossible to replace him—when Bettino trusts no one.
          "Start by getting her the fuck out the contest, Nicole.
          And gimme five ticks in a room with this jit. Go."
             "Right now?"
          "I gotta show you how?"
Bettino rises. Jane stops him—
             "Where you going, bae?"
The king looks back at his crowd.
Jane's right. He sits down.

❧

Meanwhile, Mel's adrenalized,
escorted by security down the apron steps—
plank by plank, back to the bullpen—
when Spur takes her hand, ushers her back up to the wings.   50
    Moving past
V@$T @ppe@l's loitering crew crowding the route—
notably 1DaFull, the kind of dude who stares
and don't care. Rocking headphones inside,
jamming the path. Do-rag, no need for a comb.
Versace shades à la Heavy, except imitation, Varseces.
    "Not bad, shorty…"
V@$T @ppe@l like:
        "Fuck that toy trick."
Walking ahead, reveling in the rush, Mel hears it   60
but doesn't *hear it*.
1DaFull like:
    "I'm working on it, god."
Mel passing the prompt corner, stage left
couldn't care less.

Gliding past the narrow masking flats in back:
Mel in total euphoria, Spur guiding her behind
    the proscenium
gliding to the far side of the wings, stage right.
Brick walls, counterweights, lantern lights.   70
Amidst the faint smell of ancient greasepaint,
proud musk of mothball curtains, backdrop canvases,
vaped mineral oil from fog machines.

She sees Spur send off a stagehand, clear a spot. Backstage
    lights dim,
azure hues tinting their skin tones blue. Improvised rendez-
    vous interlude.
She studies his face for a verdict:
What's it gonna be?
Feedback what she's scared to want
but knows she needs.

Spur stares back, grins:
    "Fuckin' rocked it."
She can barely control her excitement, bursts
back toward the wings, then back
to Spur in the same jolt of energy. Propelled
to a corner behind the stage, beneath a catwalk,
at the base of an emergency staircase, iron-rusted.
She puts his hand on her heart. Their eyes meet.
Mel like:
        "This must be how Billie and Lauryn
        and Nina felt after the first time—
        Ella, that first talent show at the Apollo—
        amazing, right? What an adrenal rush—
        wow—fuck a shit!"
Too loud. Stagehands swivel from the wings.
And stowaway drifters, sipping libations, redirect
    their attentions.
Spur's like: *That's great—talk lower.*
Mel in seventh heaven, on cloud nine:
        "Feels like I'm on caviar shrooms."
She takes in the cavernous confines
for the first time:

old dimmer panels, worn set dressings,
rust-edged emergency exit route map
beside the iron staircase.
Amped on nostalgia. Drunk
from performing. Geeking details:
Theater announce system speakers
placed for the benefit of those backstage—
whether Benny and the Jets,
or Derek and the Dominos, or
Sam and Dave back in the day.
Mel knows
the amp transmitted to them all—
before the place went to shit,
Valdemar used to communicate to the makers of hits,
now she's in its grip, its range, broadcasting.
They can see the last emcees onstage. Some losing their flows,
    stuck.
Others running outta breath, hard-pressed to finish.
The last one: 1DaFull dropping his rhymes,
huge headphones on his neck, imitation Versace Varseces on
    his beak,
nowhere near as good as Mel.
    "Getting dough, fucking hoes
    Pushing blow—raise the volume
    On this microphone—'bout to make
    Y'all's earbuds blow—I say
    'Hear enough?'—Y'all say
    'Well, 1Dafull…
    Fo sho!'"
Clear: the creep's fulla crap.

Spur's like:
    "So how we gonna celebrate
    after you win?"
Mel smiles, mind flashing
to celebrating with Spur-of-the-Moment.
On a balcony or a beach
overseeing the city or sea—or in Tuscany,
lights twinkling in the night air.
Toes in the sand, royal medallion chain
on her neck. Princess Pretty-Dope
kissing this dude with the taste of champagne
in her throat.
Believing a life could turn for good on a dime,
despite the things she's seen.
Prove her point to Mima, see the expression on her face
when Mel buys a magic-mad-science-shit cure for all that ails
    her queen, as rich folks do.
No more suffering. Universal debts come due.
Prove accurate her day one, Rosa, too. Hope she can see the
    esteem—wherever she is.
Can't wait for her ex-first love—Thou Who Shall Remain
    Nameless—to find out.
Traveling, touring. Full moon in Virgo. Gonna need an abacus
    to count the abundance.
Beyond safe. Basking on a yacht beside Beyoncé and a
    Basquiat, in Balenciaga, hoisting glass
Baccarat. Brunch. Beethoven on the Atmos, then Betty and
    Hov. Helipad hella rad. Luxurious.
Fantasies going there, but Mel's not about to show her hand
    to Spur:
        "You don't know I'll win—and why

would I smoke it with you if I did?"
"Because I'm a hundred-percent A1,
which is also how I know you're
gonna win. It's like a special power—"
She kisses him.

Forgets where they are.
Could listen to Fela Kuti with this cute fella—
sit cross-legged on the Marley Fest grass with this cardi-
    gan wearer;
feeling his arms around her, firm biceps.
That new mouth taste; lips, tongue, breath.
Those first touches, fingertips tingling, peach fuzz on her
    arms abuzz.
Sugarplum blushes, Pandora's box opening,
subtle scents, kicking off pheromones, laws of attraction.
(Budding career; no time for romance.)
Bodies thinking dirty. Vices. Voices vocalizing the
    nicest noises.

Stagehands and techs pass.
She pulls back. *Oops.* Glances back
toward the stage, where her heart is.
Spur hot for her—but she's hot for the contest.
    "I know a chill spot to celebrate your win—
    not far from here. Pretty-Dope, you in?"
But he gets a call on his earpiece. Listens, then:
    "Ah, fuck… Yeah, I'm comin'."
Mel recalls Spur said he puts out fires
for Heavy, says:
    "Somebody ringin' the fire alarm?"

Spur smiles, mischievous, playful:
    "When I need to be dealin'
    with this one right here."
He stays close. But she's back to business:
        "This one's gonna have to stay lit
        'til after the contest."
Spur nods, and starts to go: 200
    "You got this, Poe-ette.
    On with the show."
Colgate grin on him, fine form in motion.
Mel admires him as he goes, then turns back to the show.
Alone, hungry for a microphone. Digs in her pocket, eyeing
    the game,
rivals. She checks her bedazzled cell.
The silent icon showing.
["5 Missed Calls"]
from ["Mima"]   210
Mel stares at the message, like: *Fuck off.*

Tucks it away, glances
at the old surroundings.
Movement of emcees and stagehands, coming and going,
everything tinted cobalt. Feels like she's making it already.
Blueprint coming alive just in time. Relishes the bitter-
    sweet moment,
wishing there wasn't beef with Mima.
Mel takes it all in. Looks up,
past catwalks, rigs and bridges,   220
and spots
a
figure

slip
out
of
view
in the rafters.

Seriously, what the fuck was that?
The spectator specter again?
Or someone part of a gang?
Incognito in the indigo blank.
Like a batá drummer playing ghost notes
(rhythmic value with no discernible pitch):
Where did it go? Where did it go?
She takes a step forward, peering up
through the truss.
Curious, but hesitant to know, scanning the dark above.
Senses heightened—visualizing—ear-sight peeping the HUM
of the AMPS and offbeat hi-hats. Takes another step
under the rafters, gazing up, up, up.
BOOM! Someone
bumps past her—
Truth-Is, social media herald and co-host,
hurrying toward the stage in a beret, blazer,
bell-bottoms and platforms. Mel startled
by the local celebrity, who's like:
    "Onstage, emcee killa."
Mel like: *OMG!—you know who I am!*
Then she throws one last glance
toward the creepy rafters beyond the rigs.

Onstage, a blur of moments later,

cramped in the crush of emcees, Mel shields her eyes
from the bright lights. Eager, she sweeps her view
to Heavy's throne, sees the king staring back.
She smiles,
doesn't see his eyes—or lips—give hers dap.
Why's that?
Uneasy, Mel looks away,
focuses on the BIG BOARD listing emcees.
Soon her name is gonna need a numeral between 1-8 beside it,
    if she's to remain.
V@$T @ppe@l and his squad crowding her airspace,
with eyes on the same thing, lead bully saying ish like:
    "Sure as shit got some salt up in here tonight.
    Suckas should just hand me the crown now."
His calvary nod like drones. Eyes on Mel. Lil Bone-A-Part like:
        "Bunny's gonna get burned like candle
        wax, for fact, Jack."
    "Who's this?"
      "Pretty-Do—"
"Never mind."
V@$T struts away. Minions yodeling and giggling. The crew
    passes. The last one stops.
        "I wanna know what your name is, shorty.
        Mine's 1DaFull."
Mel holds her tongue, not getting burned again. 1DaFull
    lowers his huge headphones.
        "What's the matter? Wack emcee got
        your tongue?"
Houselights dim. The spotlight's beam
hits centerstage: Truth-Is on the mic,
alone in the circle's glow:

> "Alright, y'all, get your last votes in.
> We're locking the board in five, four,
> three, two…"
1DaFull wraps an arm around Mel; she shrugs it off.
The crowd votes on their phones.
Positions of names change on the board
—increasing speed—
slot machine, dozens of options,
Mel hoping not to roll a string of lemons.
Imagines Mima's embrace when she sees Mel's made it.
The words *I'm so proud of you, Mija,* emerging from her
     mom's mouth
when Pretty-Dope buys her old girl a miracle cure, a crib,
a whip, ice-cold bling, anything, everything. *Life's a gift.*

Meanwhile, Nicole Echo-No-Mics works her phone:
Taps "Edit"—switches "9" & "8"—taps "Save."
The BOARD LOCKS.
And the SCREEN goes BLACK.
Truth-Is still on the mic:
> "If you see your name
> in the top eight,
> step into the spotlight,
> best place on Earth."
Heavy chiming in, like:
> > "If you don't see your name,
> > better luck next time, peace out."

The king's eyes landing on Mel. She holds her breath.
Emcee forenames, surnames, and nicknames reappear on
     the board.

Mel's vision darts from rapper to rhymer.
She sees rose gold V@$T @ppe@l
with #2…
Kandela Del Fuego
with #4…
Finds herself smiling in anticipation…
But her face falls
as she sees:
Numbers 1, 3, 5, 6… and 7…
drop.
Then 1DaFull turns to Mel,
the screen behind him sporting #8 beside his name,
wise to what it means for her:
"Ouch!"

Just like that:
Out.

320

Track 7

Freestyle Freelancer

MEL DIES INSIDE
at the sight
of her number: 9.
Staggers back, losing her footing.
Voice soft, breaking, flow wasted:
    "No, no, no, no, no…"

Truth-Is like:
    "These eight advance to Round Two!"
The HERD HOLLERS.
Mel can't talk, can't breathe…
The show can't go on
without her.

But she's forced past Box Office Girl, who waves goodbye.
Sweet Lady Jane chimes in on her mic:
    "Before we move on to the next,
    let's give it up for the rest."
Cast away, Mel flounders against a tide
of eliminated emcees on a sad path back
to the permanent bullpen.

Like a chorus disseminating her hunch,
banished emcees like:
    "Nah, this is wack, yo!"
        "What the fuck, dawg!"
            "No way I don't belong!"
                "Fuckin' shit's rigged, bro!"
                    "Dropped all my chips for this shit!"
                        "Illegitimate!"
                            "What the fuck now?"
Mel sees Heavy glance her way. Her core
breaking, farther and farther astray.
This side of paradise lost.
Blue and exiled. Why not give her flowers while she can still
    smell 'em?
        "No, no, no, no, no."

She tries to break toward Heavy, her hero:
        "Yo, H! Wait up!
        Yo Majesty! His Highness!"
Bouncers box her back. Mel like:
        "You heard me flow!"
No chance, no way.

"You heard me..."
This can't be happening. She sees eliminated emcees
ahead of her booted back to the bullpen. Tries to slip out of
       the line.
A bouncer ushers her back in file,
Mel pulls out her last card:
       "I know Spur!"
The bouncer like:
    "Honey,
    you ain't the only girl."
To another bouncer:
    "More than one in every club.
    What's that gotta do with us?"
Insult to injury. Opposite of victory.
Just then, 1DaFull swoops in do-rag first,
vulture-like, hooks hold of her arm.
              "There you is. She with me, homie. Obliged,
              much respect. I'm Number Eight -
              soon to be Number One."
The bouncer like:
    "Yeah, whatev. What she say?"
Mel sees him wait for her reaction
to 1DaFull's arm on her.
She nods at the bouncer. It works. He leaves
Mel access to the wings. Green room waiting, portal open.
She sees exiled emcees: pigs to the slaughter,
groaning and moaning in the pen, broke and broken,
ghosted. Better on the opposite side of them, she thinks
as she Adidas the track.
But once past the wings, 1DaFull veers her off the path,
confiding in her like:

"Listen, listen, listen.
        Must be a bitch in the Matrix
        'cuz you was better than me, fo sho…"
Finds herself at his mercy, a plus-one, the math.
Learn it fast.
Falling down
the metaphorical staircase;
1DaFull laying it on, down the ladder, saying shit like:
        "I can help you get what you want."
Mel hearing a broken record,
and not just her heart.
        "I want back in the contest -
        got that in your top hat?"
        "Like the rabbit in your rhyme."
That tempts her attention.
        "How? You got Bugs
        Bunny on speed-dial?"
        "Top secret. Let's converse in private."
Now she sees where this is going.
A wolf who wants to fuck her pink hoodie.
Of all the times… Mel like:
        "How's spittin' with you gonna get me
        back in the Great Eight?
        Gonna gimme your slot?"
        "Better. You toke?
        Got some killer Cali.
        Global hookups and shit."
        "What about the contest?
        Gonna tell 'em 'hold on,
        be strong' like the Outkast song?"
        "Gon be fast as Dash and the Flash."

Mel not buying it.
But she sees the last of the eradicated emcees
try to bum-rush back past the apron—they get
quickly hauled out of the play,
bouncers acting like vaudeville curtain hooks,
next scene's gonna take place back out on the street.
Dead meat. Mel fearing the price of defeat.
Meanwhile, 1DaFull's like: 110
        "You want back in or what,
         shawty? This offer's goin', goin'…"
Short on options, Mel stares at him. Knowing
what he wants, what tip he's on.
       "Crystal. Let's spit.
       And make it quick."

❧

She ponders:
Could he be violent?
Regretting not having mace or a knife.
Bus locker key between her knuckles   120
all she's got to fend a predator off.
Down a long corridor, dark ceilings
with red fluorescents beating above
as Mel keeps up with 1DaFull, who's moving
past an "OUT OF SERVICE" sign hanging
on the gentlemen's room door. Downstairs
to a dim-lit lower-level corridor,
alone with the cold, yellow-coke, Edison bulbs,
hastening beneath backstage—
toward an ill-lit, musky dead end.   130
Past dressing rooms, workshops, prop departments,

glimpsing someone else's memories
of techs in black and showgirls
in robes and half-costumes, Mel sees
1DaFull's imitation Versace Varseces scan closed doors.
She says:
> "How top secret is this? Feels
> like entering Area 51."
> > "Fo sho."
No answer, that one pearl. Clear instead of crystal, crystal
   instead of clear.
Frustrating to wonder how many other girls
had to do what she was having to do
just to get a chance—
when dude's like 1DaFull just got a chance.
No lap dancing for him unless it was on *his* lap.
Shafts of AC blast from nowhere vents
and HOWL through the wind-tunnels
as 1DaFull swings open a CREAKY DOOR
labeled "WARDROBE."
Mel slows but has no choice. Steps into
> the shadows—
> > enters the darkness,
> > > hand leading the way…
> > > > touches somebody—
Ah, shit! Steps back on sawdust—
1DaFull flips a switch. Lights spark
on makeup table mirrors. And Mel sees
she's facing a cheap wool suit
on a dummy.
Surrounded by cracked looking glasses
and costumes. Wig room to the left, laundry to the right.

Workshop in a loft above.
She scoots away from the wool suit,
collecting herself from the fright.

1DaFull eyeing her like a mark:
        "Chillax, shawty. Your dreams
        are about to come true."
Between her and the door. Sparks a blunt, offers.
If she's gonna do it, might as well dim the pain,
get high—*fuck it*—defeated.
Dirt from earlier not even washed away,
not even by the rain.
She takes the Dutch, tokes. Smokes like a pro
because she is. Hands it back. Tasting the hydro.
        "So, Dash and the Flash, what
        kind of secret we spittin'?"
Defensive, wanting to own what it means,
insensitive, she gestures like a perv jester:
        "Manual secret?
        Oral secret?"
So sick of this shit, but desperate
to get on with the show—
        (sticks out her ass)
        "Booty secret?"
Ready for whatever gets her out of purgatory, when—
1DaFull whips out a small notepad
of incomplete rhymes:
        "Take a peek at these. I got some
        hot shit, too—but I'm down to listen
        if you got any ideas or clues."
WTF? Mel stares at the notepad in his hand.

Freddie Freeloader wants a freestyle freelancer?
        "You're lookin' for a ghost writer?"
    "Looking for talent… to work with."
Whoa, 180.
        "What happened to helpin' me
        get back in the contest?"
1Dafull sings:
    "THIS IS HOW WE DO IT"
Gets serious:
    "Through me."

Mel weighs her options.
Why not ask Spur?
Where he at, where the offers?
Rather not run the risk, diminish the danger of seeing
    the dude,
disappointing if he propositioned her to help him finish.
        "What you gonna do for me?"
1Dafull like:
    "You help me win this thing,
    and I'll put you on.
    You can even join my crew.
    Fuck V@$T @ppe@l—
    gonna start my own. Gonna be crunk.
    Sick of V@$T's mom managing us."
He's so confident, she almost believes him.
    "Do the math. Gonna hook you up
    with a cosign. Sittin' on mad connects.
    Producers, managers, A&Rs. Word
    is bond, boo. I'll help you. Just bet.
    With this, that, and a third. Just take

a gander at some of these punch rhymes,
    see what you can do."
Better than nothing. She takes the rhyme book.
Flips through—grimaces. *These rhymes suck.*
But she starts thinking…

Imagines moving words like pieces
on a chessboard, or a puzzle.
Strings in a theory, text   230
within new contexts, unmuzzled.
Word chains changing, morphing,
absorbing ounces of history seeping
in her psyche:
~~scratched out,~~
REPLACED,
others TRANSPOSED
from one line to
another. Reworking
a rhyme, like it's a sign,   240
each piece a musical note—
sound symbols,
syllables swinging—pauses thrusting hips and pelvises.
Resurrecting Elvises. Harmonizing with Muddy Waters.
Putting music to paper in her mind, on a roll like Jelly
    Roll Morton,
arranging and rearranging. A Radiohead Audioslave in
    her Soundgarden.
White Stripes and Black Keys. Ziggy Stardust, Dark
    Twisted Fantasy.   250
1Dafull like:
    "Oh, that's raw. Yeah, like that."

Mel finds him over her shoulder.
Overly eager, face like a boner.
        "Dope you dig. But I can't go down
        on the Muse with you lookin' over my shoulder.
        Your nose might run into her knee. It's space we need."
Dude checks his phone:
    "We got twenty minutos."
Mel in a mini-zone, flow state
parameters met:
        "Just need cinco. You can warm-up
        or somethin' 'til I get words set."
She pushes out the wardrobe's exit
with the book of wannabe punchlines,
on the hook for rhymes in need of a thump.
1Dafull calling out:
    "Clock's tickin'!"
The door shuts. Left to wait, he
starts pacing, practicing:
    "Ain't gonna be hexed by no wench
    Whatever, whateva—bash yo dome
    With a microphone or a poem—say
    'Fuck this bitch' and take ya ass home—
    no, no, wait—that sucks."
Shrugs it off, annoyed. Checks the eon
on his phone. Time to go. Undies in a twist.
    "Shit, Honey, betta hurry."
Goes to tuck the phone away,
when a ROUGH, MANGLED HAND
GRABS HIS WRIST.

Track 8

Beat Drop

OUTSIDE THE WARDROBE door:
SCREAMS PENETRATE
through the old wood
and dissipate down the corridor—
lonely, blanketed
by MUSIC FROM THE SHOW'S INTERMISSION seeping
down into the theater's hollows,
one of Heavy's golden hits:

"…Front page Miami Herald and Sun Sentinel
Local hero going seminal—global—Heavy Reign!
King conquering kingdoms on all sides of Ecuador
Used to catch Heavy at Seminole casinos, stacking several…"
Meanwhile, upstairs on the backstage level,
in a red-lit hall, unaware, Mel works
on 1DaFull's lines,

brick wall, "SILENCE" sign, under a dim bulb—
sound of MUSIC BLARING from the stage,
machine gun salvo—
just playing with ideas, praying
this helps her DOA career,
when a large shadow creeps across the page.

Fear startles Mel back against the wall.
Face-to-face with Heavy, her hero, and Nicole Echo-No-Mics,
his fedora-clad, silver-haired, Diddy-like sister.
Awed.
Forgetting about 1DaFull's book
of rhymes, hands falling to her side.
The king all like:
     "Sweet verse."
Close enough to smell the sweat beneath his cologne.
Musk. Mel so struck, she's thinking: *what?* Says:
     "Verse?"
Wishes she'd rehearsed for this convo.
          "*Freestyle* you just dropped."
Echo-No-Mics crosses herself, warding off some curse.
Mel feeling like she's gotta be dreaming,
close to the king, fumbling words,
su-su-suddenly stuttering, (much respect)—
          "Did-did-did you like it?"
Sp-sp-sputtering. Flipping her lid.
MUSIC from the intermission SMOTHERING
the subterranean sound, suffocating shit,
with the likes of:
     "Heavy Reign!
     The forecast, feel the downpour

Fucking up so many tracks, actually
Caught something
STD from a foursome with
A mixtape, a CD, and an MP3
'How can it be, G?' Said, 'Y'all tellin' King!'"

Heavy pressing the subject:
    "Where'd you get your freestyle from?"
Heavy talking to her, you heard?
Stepping outside herself
to observe the absurd:
the legendary voice aimed at her.
    "C'mon, don't be putting us on."
Mel trying to get her head straight, act her weight.
        "The freestyle? I just came up wit—"
    "No need to front, lil momma."
Flashes a big smile, gold and white-gold grillz,
brilliant, emcee charmer.
Seduce snakes to dance with a glance—
twerk,
work—
tap dance for acceptance,
Mel overwhelmed—
this is her chance.
But it's getting awkward.
        "I'm not lyin'."
    "Verse just came outta
    thin air, right, huh?"

She hesitates. King so confident,
making her doubt her confidence.
Vibes ballooning tense, about to pop. Heavy's eyes incensed.

He bully-prods her in the chops, interrogating like a cop.
        "Really, I came up with it.
        How can I prove it to you?
        What am I supposed to do
        if y'all don't believe my truth?"
Heavy and Echo-No-Mics stay silent,
letting her hang herself—Mel aghast,
pondering what they think they know she don't.
Waiting for her to swerve to another tale that's tall.
        "I have been writing rhymes since
        I was five. Earlier than that, actually—"
    "You ain't heard the song before?"
Can't tell if the king's bluffing
or he knows something she don't.
        "Can't be yours—
        I know 'em all."
    "Wipe ya mouth, and brown from your nose.
    Fucking flattery ain't finna get you out this mess."
        "I ain't done nothing wrong.
        Rhymes come from somewhere else,
        you know? Collective unconscious,
        Muse, God—who knows. I don't.
        Same with that freestyle flow
        Maybe came from one of 'em ghosts
        hanging 'round the shadows."
That gives them pause.
The BEAT STALLS.
During the halt,
they hear 1DaFull's SCREAMS (without stop)—
and then the BEAT DROPS—BREAKING
BACK LOUDER than before. CROWD CHEERING

and HOLLERING through the walls, energy echoing
down the hall.
Mel, Heavy and Echo-No-Mics exchange a look.
What the fuck was that, y'all?   110

In a flash, the passageway passes away,
splashing in and out of shadows,
Mel dashing through the corridor,
painting chiaroscuro,
trailing Echo-No-Mics and Heavy
converging on the wardrobe—
Mel compelled to follow,
dragged by an invisible harpoon—
sees them turn the handle,
step through the threshold,   120
but stop. Heavy like:
        "Ah, fuck."
Mel catches up. And he pushes her inside
to the scene of the crime.

In the FLICKERING
WARDROBE ROOM LIGHT
from makeup mirror bulbs,
amidst scattered moth-eaten
and battered costumes and piss and shit perfume,
she finds—   130
1DaFull's cracked phone face-up on the sawdust floor…
ON THE SCREEN:
the VOLUME BAR
                ALL

THE
WAY
UP
TO
THE
TOP   140

PLUS, MAXIMUM BASS MODE ON.
Mel's gaze
follows the bandwidth from the source,
through the chord,
to the headphones
duct-taped to 1DaFull's head…
His eyes bulging,
face sandwiched
BETWEEN the PHONES:
SOUND in full gear, MUFFLED   150
by stereo-blaster earmuffs
rocking his dead skull,
brain fried…
blood leaking from his ears, buds blown,
spilled scarlet
vibrating from
the sonic disturbance.
No bandage can fix this.
Hands and wrists bound
by polyethylene,   160
bloody, stiff as a figurine. Straight
outta Halloween, came a month early.
Aural guillotine,
more suited for a silver screen or pulp magazine.
Can still smell the joint they smoked,

spent roach on the floor.
Mel absorbing it all, still holding
his rhymes, going stiff, like:
        "Fuck a shit…"

Track 9

F**k a S**t

MEL FEELS PALE-SICK at the sight.
Stale vomit spit storms up
her windpipes. Clogging up,
innards in her body frosted like an iced lens.
View fogging up: a dead body hard to process.
Pushing back progress, she heads for the entrance—
exit; can't even get her head straight.

Heavy stops her flat. Shuts the door.
LOCKS the latch.
Nicole Echo-No-Mics snaps a look at him, freaked,
like: *It's a trap. Don't lock us in here with this shit.*
Fedora about to fly off her lid.
Heavy another kind of phased, like he's seen worse things—
bearing down on Mel, towering over her:

"Who the fuck are you, girl?"
Backs her into a makeup table mirror
tipping back and forth against the wall,
boudoir lamp toppling to the floor.
Glass shatters across Mel's Adidas
paws as she barely gets out an answer: 20
          "I was in the contest—"
Zeus-thunder in the king's voice:
     "Don't be a smart-ass.
     Who sent you?"
Echo-No-Mics chimes in, scratching her scarred cheek,
like an itch she can't cinch:
               "What kind of brujería
               you bring here, girl?"
Surprised, Mel stares
at Echo-No-Mics in the flickering light,   30
considers the multicolor-bead chains,
even if Nicole Echo is thinking insane,
making Mel for a witch. Better to be called a bitch.
          "Me, momma?
          We on the same team.
          Ghosts, spells, whatever—
          seems like they been threaded
          into this theater's seams."
Mel just letting her know how it is.
Echo-No-Mics throws a glance at Heavy, like there's more.   40
               "What was that about lyrics
               coming from a ghost?"
Heavy nudges Echo-No-Mics aside:
     "Get outta here with that shit talk, Nicole."
But his sister's not letting it go, like:

"I ain't playing, Bettino.
We need to cleanse
with an *ebo*—
right now, before shit blows."
    "I'm done tellin' you, Nicole."
Mel peeks back at the body,
turns away, sick, realizing:
Still holding his notebook. Shit. Drops
it—spine split open.
1DaFull a rare one, like her, who didn't keep rhymes in the
    Notes app
on his phone. Mel like:
        "Anybody gonna call Five-O?"
Heavy like:
    "Hell no."
        "But he's…"
    "And we got no permit to be here.
    And the door money.
    And backdoor Cuban caretakers
    that can't be trusted.
    This be on us."
Mel sees Echo-No-Mics pull the closest cloth
off a rack: a glittery red dress—
the kind Donna Summer would have
and wear, a stunner at the disco fair—
but Echo-No-Mics covers the body instead—
without looking at it.
Barely enough to cloak the face and torso.
Pumas pointing up. Imitation Versaces smashed
on the cement. Like trash.
Echo-No-Mics crosses herself, kisses the beads;

Mel knows the whole routine.
Echo nods to Heavy, leaves. The king like:
    "And we finish things."
Heavy draws a .45 Glock, presses it
to Mel's cheek—cold steel bringing the heat.
Snatches her backpack. Checks it. Pulls
out a handful of Golden Age cassettes
and the Walkman. Books.
Sees the tape inside the Sony
is one of his: *Raw-Y'all Golden Hits & Anthems.*
Sees Miles in the water bottle:
    "That a fucking fish?"
        "That's Miles.
        Y'know,
        like the Davis."
    "Who gives a flying fuck?"
He tosses the backpack aside. Mel like:
        "I don't know who did this. I swear."
Heavy keeps the gun up on her,
as if she's some kind of monster.

Close enough to see the amethysts shine
on his gold and white-gold grillz,
and light refract off the earring pinned to his nose,
and his glistening pores, iconic tats on forearms,
the sweat-wet silk collar of his purple guayabera,
the tiny fabric hairs on his royal suede loafers by Qüero,
    not Clarks.
But most of all, the Raw-Y'all Records medallion
at iris-level, calling to Mel like a Bat-signal.
So close but so far.

Far enough to see she needs to get started talking:
        "I'm your biggest fan. Since the first time
        I heard "Manifest the Best," "Heavy Reign,"
        "Reign All Day"—man—I just wanted
        to be half as good as you. Read your Wiki
        a million times. Every rhyme, every interview.
        All true. Would never dare play you for a fool."
Clear from the switch on his face,
she tickled his clitoris with that one.
Got him thinking,
drawing back the gun.
Ego-stroking, Mel keeps on:
        "I know all those stories
        about how you stay on top
        by putting on new artists,
        just like all the legendary smartest:
        Miles, The Duke, Art Blakey, Dr. Dre,
        the list goes on.
        I'm a total King Heavy junkie."
Through his dark Versace frames, she sees the outline of his
    eyes catch
on something below her neckline: gold-embossed
    imprint peeking
from behind her hoodie's V-line. Heavy lowers the sweat-
    er's zipper
with the barrel of his Glock, parts the sides with the tip
and reveals her King Heavy halter top.
        "You a Stan."
                "Nah, just appreciate the craft."
Heavy studies her in the flickering
luminescence. She stiffens,

steeling herself for whatever's next.
Can still hear the HUM EMANATING
from 1DaFull's headphones   140
beneath the glittering dress.
The next song louder than the last,
imagine that.
The gun barrel retracts
from between Mel's cotton layers.
Heavy turns off 1DaFull's tune,
keeping album-cover eyes on her:
        "Tell me this, biggest fan:
        You wanna fuck the king up?
        Cause problems?"   150
                "Hells no."
        "You swear to keep shut
        'bout this… gang hit?"
                "Yeah, yes—for sure."
Way too late to quit.
"What about that 'freestyle?'"
                "OMG, I swear, straight off the top of the dome."
Heavy deep-thinking, responding with:
        "Then consider yo'self lucky tonight
        'cuz I'm finna let you go home."   160
He tosses Mel her backpack—

She catches it. Then:
                "No."
She glances at the covered body, flinches.
                "He was Number Eight. I'm Number Nine.
                I should take his spot. That's only right."
Scared shitless, she fights to mask it,

appear confident. Heavy like:
    "You can get the fuck outta here."
But Mel knows:
To make a name you gotta stake a claim.
        "I paid to play. I deserve—"

Heavy takes her arm, tosses her far,
against a rack of costumes—
feathers and frills spill—re-draws
his gun. Increases her desperation.
Heavy like:
    "The fuck you do. Fresh-faced jit.
    Should've just got the fuck out,
    skate back to the crib,
    cried to your momma
    or some shit. Wanna
    come with terms. Think
    you know me. You don't
    know shit. No clue
    what I had to do to—or get through—to get here,
    and no clue what I'll do to stay on."
A KNOCK interrupts.
Mel hears Nicole Echo-No-Mics say: "It's me."
And Heavy opens up, violet-tinted Versaces still fixed on Mel.
    "You didn't lock the fuckin' door
    when you left."
His sister replies on the far side, obscured:
        "Don't be trying to put that on me.
        Need a key to lock it from outside, right?"
Echo-No-Mics returning with Spur,
carrying trash bags and electrical tape,

forgetting to close the door, when they see Mel
in the path of Heavy's Glock, on the verge of joining 1DaFull
	on the floor—

200

Mel and Spur exchanging surprises:
		"Spur!"
				"Poe-ette?"
Echo-No-Mics like:
				"You know her?"
And Heavy:
		"Yo, shut the fuckin' door!"
Heavy and Echo-No-Mics (who's locking the latch)
	now watching
Spur, who gives Mel a face that aims to calm

210

her nerves. Her hoping what he says
doesn't make matters worse.
				"Put the gat away, H. She's good peeps.
				Dope, like her name. Nothin' this fucked up
				would ever occur because of her. I mean, look
					at her."
Listen to this. Patronizing unintentional.
He regards the remains, then the trash bags and tape.
				"And on a more immediate topic:
				I'm not gonna try and hide

220

				no body. This is cray. Don't
				know who did it—or if they're even still here.
				And what if the cops show?
				Can't pay 'em all off.
				And they ain't gonna trust, or side, with us.
				I got college in two months."
Heavy like:
		"Not if you don't stop actin' like a lil bitch."

113

Spur like:
>   "Nah, nah, nah—don't do that.   230
>   You can't. We had a deal."
He spins to Echo-No-Mics, and she's like:
>   "Wanna go to college?
>   Hide this damn body."
Then Mel hears herself say:
>   "I know where to hide it."

She sees them all stare at her,
struggling to take her measure
as Heavy keeps her pressed against
hangers of cotton and polyester.   240

Feeling the pressure,
she eyes his necklace medallion treasure.
(Like a holy grail to her.)
She nods, confirming.
>   "I've read all about this place—
>   from even before when you played.
>   They built it on top of an old jail.
>   Never demolished the cells. But I bet
>   y'all no one ever goes down there.
All of them stunned by her suggestion.   250
>   "So now that I told you where
>   to hide the body,
>   can I be down with the crown,
>   and have back my *shotty*?"

Nicole Echo-No-Mics trying to read her
as Spur grows wary. Pride a bit wounded, too.

Even a fool would see it in those irises and pupils.
Silence, heavy like the king.
But Heavy laughs, holsters the gun,
lights another Cuban, far from done:
 "Tellin' ain't helpin'.
 But…
 if you go hide this fool's body,
 you can take his place,
 Number Eight."
She thinks *he thinks*
she must have a mystical thing going on
full swing,
even though he's cynical.
Heavy hard to read in gold and white-gold and
 purple minerals.
Maybe he's intrigued by the lyrical.
Maybe sees a glimmer of the star
his energy could make her be—
the genesis planetary, legacy pivotal.
Maybe just curiosity of who she is,
figuring Pretty-Dope's holding out—
can't kick her to the ground, stage door closing
on her bottom.
Nah, gotta keep her around—
wanna understand the why, what, and where.
Plus she's got a brass pair.
Good enough for her. At least she's there.
Offer on the table.
Body on the floor.
Makeup lights like celestial forms
twinkling in her optics.

MUSIC THUMPING
in her mind
like a VENTRICLE PUMPING the divine.   290
Whatever it takes. Tonight's the night.

Graffiti Labyrinth

"SO COLLEGE, HUH?"

"Sure,
if we don't all get killed
or locked up."

Mel's flashlight app probes
the darkness below,
illuminating rusted iron steps
swallowing
light into a
black hole.
Oh, hell.

Damned, Mel might as well get that soul strut shuffling
from the lower-level landing near the wardrobe.
    "C'mon."
Spur holds the head-end
of 1DaFull's new costume:
body wrapped—Donna Summer dress
tucked with rhyme book and smashed imitation shades
in a package made of trash bags tied with tape on the ends.
A broken medley.
Almost broken, Melody
meets Spur's wary gaze across the fragments.
Oya, the Goddess of Death and Wind,
who 1DaFull's gone over with—
but Oya seems to have only taken some of him.
Mel's been seeing 1DaFull's spirit
ever since she made the deal with Heavy,
fishing for a record deal.
Now the spirit of the dead's there.
Threadbare. Dead stare. Golden-staircase year.
Do-rag looking like a poop bag.

Mel came to move bodies but not like this.
Crosses herself without thinking, chilled to the bone marrow
by both body and ghost. Steeling herself for the deed.
Desperate to succeed, however it be.
Too late to get a degree. Says:
    "Let's do this fast."
Asks, then arm-squeezes him to listen:
But Spur's on alert, he keeps saying 1DaFull's killer
could still be around, seeking another victim.
He's pissed at Heavy for not ending the show.

Wants to protect her—that Mel knows, but bro's gotta let that
    go,
stop cock-blocking her immediate goal.
Spur, hefting the corpse, like:
        "If 1DaFull's this heavy,
            can't imagine what H's fat ass is like."
        "Banish the thought. And hurry up.
        We gotta get back in time."

Beginning the descent, Mel
holds the leg-end and the light
while Spur hauls from the head-end.
Things still tense. Cut the air with a cleaver.
Plus every step's a challenge. Grunting
from the weight,
like dragging IKEA
furniture, furnishing her with more urgency:
    "Hurry up…"
        "You can be really fucking frustrating,
            know that? There's an 800-pound dead
            elephant in the room. Want me to say it?
            Fine. This ain't the way to break in, Poe-ette."
    "What exactly ain't—"
Mel loses her grip on the body,
and Spur loses his, and—

1DaFull's body TUMBLES
DOWN
    the stairs—
THU-THUMP, THU-THUMP,
THU-THUMP, THU-

50

60

70

CRACK!
Hear the SKULL SPILT
at the base.

❧

Race down
to the second lower level.
Catching up to the body, Mel and Spur
reach the dark, humid underground of the theater. Unnerved.
The head-end of the trash bag soaked in blood. No one gonna
carry that end.
Mel like:
"How 'bout you hold on tighter?
And I ain't as green as you think.
Life's a bitch, and a dick.
I know the clique."

Not wanting to hear a response, Mel pans her flashlight,
revealing:
Cement floors. Rusty pipes. Tight walls.
Dank—and not the good kind.
Ancient cells with dust so thick, light casts a mist when it
shines through it.
Intricate. Deep underground.
Once water-tight concrete box like a claustrophobic, laby-
rinth garage.
Limestone, sand, and mud. Tunnels and turns. Blueprints
a blur.
If walls could talk, they'd say they were watching.

Her source beam hits empty spray cans, used tips, and old
    faded graff, widening 2D shadows.
Desaturated paint wall-to-wall. Getups, pieces, characters,
    blockbusters, wildstyles, for sure.
Works all mixed. By the EKA Crew and affiliates:
Lack76, Plet92, Tank, June, Forge, 71Carlito, Six—tags
    unfurling paths dated last millennium:
Ject, T, Brett, Dee, Fleck, Nico, Nissim, Nome the Gr8, Ki
    Rage, Phil-B, Felix, Israel J, WES2,
Dae1, A-Rok, E-Roc, Dirt, Ditter, Erik, G-Lob, Twinz, Mor,
    Poe, Fesko, ResQ, Lenny, Leenos, Gerry, Kerry, Alan,
    BigMatt, Catfish, Oil, War, Tase, Jenny, Karla, Sosa, Olga,
    Stephanie, Reb,
Skem, Giselle, Bebo/Beba, T-Bird, X, Michelle, C-Tan, Lou,
    Liv, Tif, Miguel, Maritza, Mabel, Sara, Sab Shan, Sady,
    Gloria, Tati, Yaci, Toni, Doodie, Barb, Chanty, Bev, Red,
    Ju-C, Mildred, Pricilla, Elba, Rosie, Ro, Juli, Chris, Pilly,
    Jack137, Render, nastasja79, Luna, E-Stef LaMorena,
THA LOWE$T 37 ♥s THA REAL$T 4,
Dynamite, JustInTime, Rob from the Mob, and others too,
    like Flavor Savorz and Hell Razorz,
& Starsky, Amber, Susana, Mandy, Nancy, Amy, Sylvie, David,
    Dennis, Laz, Edwin, Betsy,
Saul M, Ped3, Cia, Mia, Cristian, Camela, Pinto, Nanny,
    Jan!ce—kaleidoscopic graffiti objects, including free agent
    VIPs: Steampunk, Cheryl, Nick, Nahdia, Nahidy, Liz,
    Lysi, Lauren, RMS, Deum, Dream, Samer, Alison, Lyndia,
    Frances, BTW, Addamys27, Kristy, and 12-Ounce Drip.
Edison & Charity. And then some random things: "Glitch,"
    "Sick," "Bitch"—
some of it like some stoned tagger numbered it,

smeared, several cell numbers flipped:
#5, #7, #6… Spur like:
> "This is cray. We can't do this.
> I'm not carrying it another inch.
> Gonna go up and tell 'em. Forget that."
"What about college? You bluffin'."
> "Not if it means more earbuds busting."

"Fine, I'll do it myself."
Stepping around rat crap,
junkie needles, and crumpled Krylon spray cans—
cracked glass and fossilized condoms
crunching under her Adidas and his Clarks—
Mel grabs the body-bagged rapper. Sees 1DaFull's spirit
walking along beside the husk.
Judging her from beyond this realm.
On his way to an unmarked grave,
not even paved.
Great.
Just the kinda guilt she's seeking to traffic in—
not—
no fuckin' way—wish it would go away.

Her beam cast over bars and cages,
following numbers escalating.
Hide this body, get back and win—
all her instincts, still: can't help thinking
Spur's Tyler-the-Creator cardigan is gonna smell
like 1DaFull's piss and shit after this.
> "These ain't people
> you wanna do dirt with."

"Heavy is exactly who."
    "Buyer beware."
"If you hate workin' for him
so much, why are you even here?
And how you get them on the hook for college?"
    "Don't front like you ain't figured it out."
"Internship? What you spittin?"
    "Because he's my uncle."
"Whoa, roll that tape back. Heavy's
your uncle? Nicole Echo-No-Mics is your—"
    "Nicole. Yeah.
    C'mon, girl,
    stop fronting—"
"I'm not! Straight fact. How
was I supposed to know?"
Dude probably thinks that's why she kissed him—
when his whole positive vibe was in her system.
    "Boy, you been in the shadows."
        "All intentional.
        Point is: I'm starting school
        in the fall. Gonna learn to code.
        Wanna build something real—even if it's digital,
        instead of just cleaning up after shows.
        My family's messes always be hectic."
"Boo-fuckin-hoo.
I need a fuckin' chance.
One goddamn beat break.
Hiding this boy's body is the closest I've been."

⁊

Her beam finds an unfinished piece

beside a mangled character:
giant blood-clotted eye blotted, veins bulging,
letters illegible, all drips and paint chips…
then no more graffiti.
Mel in a hurry for more reasons than one:
    "No more graff marks the spot -
    should be far enough."
Spur not debating for once:
        "Fine. Get this over with."
They hear METAL SNAP—turn the light back—
see a trail of blood
from the cracked-skull drag
leading into the shadows
from which they came.
Nothing else.
Endless numbered cells.

Mel sets down 1DaFull's remains as Spur regards the body,
unaware of its spirit standing near him. He SPARKS
    his phone.
Two digital torches between them. Mel seeing more of
    the place
only makes matters worse. Rat carcasses. And raccoon roadkill
    or some shit—
not peering closer, already scarred as it is. She crosses
    1DaFull's vessel
with last rites, too late. Hoping this frees his spirit from
    her path.
Probably too late for that, too.
Spur like:
        "My uncle doesn't care

about putting on nobody.
Don't believe the hype
or let him sell you otherwise.
When people stopped buying
his shit, sayin' he fell off,   220
he went and started finding artists
to 'manage.' Didn't do shit
for most of them, 'cept collect
fees. Even ripped that prize
chain off from that reality show
made by Jermaine Dupree,
you know the one."
Mel exits into the cellblock:
    "You mad fibbin'."
    "I seen it."   230
Spur follows her out, heading back
the way they came. Numbers
decreasing: #13, #12, #11, #10…
    "He knighted plenty of peeps."
    "Name one who's still on."

Mel doesn't like what she's hearing,
wishes there was a door to disappear.
Avoids stepping on the trail of 1DaFull's blood.
The two light beams cross as they probe
the cramped arteries of the dying theater.   240
Mel desperate to preserve her mental model:
    "He turned down distribution deals
    with Aftermath and Def Jam just 'cuz
    he doesn't need 'em."
        "Bullshit. No such thing happened."

Spur still going on:
     "I know my mom loves me, but
     she protects Heavy like he's her firstborn.
     What he hasn't put up his nose,
     he's dropped at the strip club.
     Now, this contest is the latest hustle.
     That fucking NittyGritty app—that's him.
     Next month he'll run another
     one of these. Anoint the next one
     and out with the last. Believe that."
Mel struggles to soak that all in.
   "Why weren't you warning me earlier,
   Edgar Allan Poe Fellowship of the Arts?"
     "I was wrong. Thinking with my Richard.
     I'm sorry. I mean it. Heavy's poison.
     You name it:
     belladonna, nightshade,
     arsenic, old lace."
   "It'll be different with me."
     "Told ya you were green.
     Dangerous thing to be, Poe-ette;
     telling you for your own good."
   "I ain't fuckin' green, olive, teal, lime, or—"
She cuts herself off
when she hears GLASS CRUNCH
behind them. They glance back,
cast weak light from
their phones, see…

Nothing but darkness. Mel like:
   "You ain't funny, rat."

Line numbers in margin: 250, 260, 270

They listen.
Hear the GROUND DISTURBED…
dirt and debris upturned.
CRUNCH. CRUNCH.
"Rat with size-twelve boots."
CRUNCH. CRUNCH. CRUNCH.
Ready to run, they discern something large…
some *thing*…
moving… *CRUNCH. CRUNCH. CRUNCH.*
Through the shadows…
Stalking toward them…
With long claws and a shiv—

Track 11

Shiv

N O, A BIG-ASS shank!

They run, dip—
zip like lemon seeds pinched
between fingers, shoot, jumping coffee beans—
pushing deeper into the cellblock, past graffiti-glyphs,
    rabbit-rigged,
stammering, scrambling, tearing through the
    pitch-black labyrinth—
Mel can't hear a goddamn thing over her
    PANICKED BREATHING.

Gasping, she turns a corner, hits a dead end past the bend.
    Shit!
Realizes she's separated from

"Spur!"
Worried for him,
        she scans the walls.
No graffiti. No numbers. Lost.
Hears FOOTSTEPS
GROWING CLOSER…
        "Spur?"   20

Strange GURGLING GROWLS,
as if from another world,
pierce
and rip
the damp silence.
She spots a hole
in the wall, large enough
for a body.
Goes through it,
into another cell—   30
her leg gets stuck—she pulls on her limb,
stumbles, falls in,
keeps her footing, then trips.
Her palms land
on something damp and sticky.
Ill, ill, ill—and not the good kind.
She rises, shines the light
on her hands:
Lady Macbeth. Baptized in red.

Disgusted, she almost gags.   40
Wipes her front paws
on the crumbling wall. Glances back

to see where the blood came from,
sees she tripped over 1DaFull.
Lost in the labyrinth. *Fuck, fuck, fuck.*
Springs out of the cell. Her light beam
barely illuminating—
reaches an intersection. Veers
right—
    CRASHES into a
        STEEL RAILING.
            Her phone springs
                from her fingers—
                    clatters across the floor.

She darts to retrieve it—her Adidas slip
on shattered glass,
    the ground shifts
        under her feet;
            she falls
                to the damp concrete.

Light just out of reach,
beam aimed away, swallowed
into the shadows.

A GROWL GURGLES behind her.

Cornered, she turns back. There it is:

        The GHOSTLY,
        HULKING
        FIGURE

towers over her—

mangled paws; rotten claws; eyes, red orbs;

something monstrous;

opaque; hard to fathom.

She shuts her eyes; cringes, terrified.
Palms pressed into crumbles of concrete,
starting to bleed.

An UNCOMFORTABLE SILENCE,
like the air was sucked out.
Mel's SHALLOW BREATHING
consumed by the
v o i d.

Sour smell, like death. Metallic, copper stench.
Then, a low, WET, GROTESQUE MOAN
BUILDS...
Like it's on top of her...
Spectral, unbearably close...
Then—

A VOICE she recognizes as Truth-Is hums
over a backstage announce system speaker, distant:
> *"Alright, y'all, time for Round Two!*
> *Where our emcees at?! I'm feeling*
> *these flows - how 'bout y'all?"*
The air decompresses as fast as it tensed.
Mel OPENS HER EYES...

It's gone. Like it vaporized

131

into fog, toked up by the dark.

Mel hypnotized by fright.

Slowly, she rises, relieved to be alive,
in the clear.
Retrieves her light… Then she's SLAMMED
from the side
into the railing, SCREAMS—
sees Spur,
relief and fear contemplating her fate,
competing to lead her—
Spur steps back like: *It's me,*
hushed, ushering:
       "C'mon, c'mon, c'mon."
She turns back
to the railing, casts light
on it, reveals a rusted staircase.

⌖

3.2 seconds later, they propel themselves
into a dark, cramped jungle of lights, mics, and backdrops.
They stumble,
pull down a posse of mannequins
and wigs.
Shut the door. LOCK it. Push a prop table
against it. Spur adrenalized,
future engineer on a path to patch exceptions,
making a superstitious exemption, like:
       "It's still fucking here.
       What the fuck is that *thing?*

Doesn't seem human. Fuck!
This is so crazy! You okay?"
She doesn't know how to answer—
just holds him close, feels his kiss on her dome,
her brow, her throbbing temples.
Lets him caress her face, taken
by genuine concern, hard-earned,
sharing something vulnerable and raw:
what the two of them saw.   130
Lips locked faster than they know it,
no invitation, no future guaranteed,
instincts leading them to show it;
squeezing, breathing each other's souls in,
emotions on a private beach,
out of evil's reach, maldición be gone quick.

Slowly pull away,
closer than before.
Flash their lights, see
they came in through a backdoor   140
to a backroom
connected to the wardrobe.
Traces of 1DaFull's earbud blood
still on the floor, caught
in the still-flickering light
of makeup-table bulbs.
The gravity of the horror pulling them
off the beach—life a bitch, slick trick,
Mel back to biz, trying to cover up this shit:
    "That didn't just happen."   150
        "Shouldn't have, but it did.

We need to split—telling Mom and H:
    time to dip."
Mel blocks his path to the main door, needing to
    nix mediation:
    "We can't tell. Not no one. Minus zero."
Even if he's not buying, she's still selling:
    "We just gotta make sure no one comes down
    to the underground."
        "Yo, you gotta hear yourself."
"All hell's gonna explode loose if you tell. No need
to carpet bomb the contest. This is my shot."
        "There'll be other options.
        Right now, you need to run the other way."
"I can't. Believe me. I been
the other way. It's why I ran
this way. Desperate. Ashamed.
Give it to the end. I'll tell 'em
with you then. Right after I win."
        "You ain't heard a word I said!"
"I'm begging you."
Spur conflicted
when Heavy comes through
the house speaker system:
        "Pretty-Dope and Lil Bone-A-Part,
        get y'alls asses up
        on this stage.
        Battle's on, bitches."
Disembodied voice
reminding her it's time
to diss somebody's noise.
She opens the door:

"See? It's almost over.
Don't tell me you never done
somethin' like this before,
    Mr. Puttin'-Out-Fires-For-Heavy."
Spur holds his pose,
but something beneath the surface
is going on, she knows.
Bro looks butthurt over her words.
        "Nah. New low,"
            Spur's quote, stepping out past her:
        "Know what—
            dig your own grave."
The vibe they once had now passed,
lost in the past.
And with that *fuck you*, he's gone.

Track 12

Yoruba Beads

BODY MOVING TO her goal,
soul aching over bro—
    trying to forget him—
she flies through the corridor
she knows too well,
to the stairwell, up
the steps, double-timing it:
up the stairs, reaches
the hallway to the stage—contest beckoning,
but rose gold V@$T @ppe@l and his clique
crowd her route—
roaming emcees and entourage,
punching their hands with their fists
like greasers in that Prince purple flick.
Flashing rose gold grillz with platinum fangs.

Cracking knuckles and scowls,
acting primed and ready to start a row—
or a fracas—
facades wrong if they think she's gonna fuckin' back up.

Must've overcrowded the green room   20
down the hall to the stage, ate all the Cuban food—
Mel can smell the remnants of arroz con pollo (and ensalada
    de aguacate)
as V@$T @ppe@l's crew eyes her with an attitude,
not cool, their leader like:
    "Calling your name."
Red fluorescents coating the tension.
Mel can hear the show beyond them,
DJ mixing Heavy's hits with chop and screw.
Determined, she goes to detour past   30
them. But V@$T @ppe@l deters her with a hip and shoulder,
baritone clone droning on, asking:
    "Where's 1DaFull?"
Mel slow to lie, finally like:
        "Who?"
No one buying it. Coming off like a fool. V@$T @ppe@l
    eyeing her
with an even more not-cool attitude, sucking a vape like he's
    got her on tape.
    "My whoadie. The playa   40
    whose space you takin'."
Lil Bone-A-Part chugging a 32 of OE
like syrup, platinum grillz snagging a glint,
showdown-at-dawn swagger like Clint,
can't tell if the slant's because he's drunk:

> "I was supposed to be schoolin'
> 1Da in Round One.
> Now, I'm gonna be schoolin' you, boo.
> Next match, WWE, WWF, can't match."

Mel like:

> "By all means then,
> let's get this show on the way,
> the express, the road.
> We runnin' late as it is, bro."

Again, tries to move past them. They box her in—
V@$T @ppe@l exhaling vapor, getting the vapors, going
    off about:

> "Echo-No-Mics is sayin'
> '1DaFull's out of the contest'—
> just up and left—like poof
> from the emcee booth.
> Now, I know that ain't true.
> He ain't ask for permission."

V@$T @ppe@l's name spelled out in rhinestone
on his rose gold grillz, glinting like Bone-A-Part's,
up in her natural. His violet-tinted corneas trace the
    gold embossing
of the Heavy halter top under her hoodie. Mel meeting his
    gaze, like:

> "That put him in line for a spankin'?
> No wonder you're upset."

Bone-A-Part laughs to himself, spitting
OE, cheap malt and barley, $2.25 a liter.
Mel tries to keep going, Adidas crossing cracks,
but V@$T and his crew don't budge,
lead bully-like:

"Oh, funny wanna flex now?"
        "You know, fronts'll make your teeth fall out."
"Where'd you even fucking come from? You
ain't 305, 786, or no shit. What crew you rep?"   80
Mel getting pangs
in her stomach 'bout where this is going,
hoping the sweat forming on her forehead ain't showing,
having to hold her ground to survive 'cuz that's what it's like.
Slim kid 'bout to catch a fat lip, Mel can't keep runnin' away
        like Imani, Romye, and the rest:
                "I rep one-two-three
                get outta my face
                with your bullshit."
V@$T offended by what she said, about to get dropped, but   90
        distracted, like:
        "That blood?"
Mel glances at her palms.
Fights her disgust,
improvises:
                "Krylon.
                Girl's gotta make her mark
                one way or another."
Defiantly, she wipes her hands
on her cheeks like war paint—even though it's freaking nasty.   100
Covering her fear. Nothing to see here.

Heavy appears at the end of the hall,
way-pissed, all-about-business.
The king wraps ringed fingers around her arm,
signals Lil Bone-A-Part to follow along—with the flick of
        a wrist—

leads them away—seems like the show is still on.
V@$T @ppe@l doing enough to make sure Mel hears:
    "Thirsty Stan 'bout to get dragged."

✍

Moving fast, past old posters, framed sepia photos,   110
autographed walls: thespians, performers,
other-era legends judging Mel
with their eyes, whole fucking place haunted.
                Past the green room derby of debauchery,
                    unaffiliated emcees and groupies
                    partaking in a marathon of vices:
endless ye-yo stanzas, Coca-A-Cola lines.
Drinks spilled
on a tabletop and not even missed,
next to half-eaten Cubano sandwiches and pan con lechón,   120
Molly in the house—popped in a mouth,
and some other Molly popping out a blouse.
Mel sees Heavy shut the door trying not to arouse
the Cuban mom and pop chaperones, and their Nike-
    clad sons,
who escaped the Revolution, commiserating down the hall.
Mel keeping up with the king, speeding up, increas-
    ing momentum,
when Lil Bone-A-Part slows the roll:
        "Ayo, I gotta drain the lizard, OG."   130
Mel points at the 32-ounce OE bottle he's got:
            "Walk and chew gum."
        "Can't rap with a full bag, yo Highness."
Heavy checks his Cartier watch, dealing with children:
    "Hurry the fuck up."

140

Lil Bone-A-Part scampers, holding his designer khakis up.
Once he's is out of sight, and they're kind of alone,
Heavy tosses her his Gucci towel:
     "Take your sweet fuckin' time,
     come back with blood
     all up your face.
     Seemin' like a Seminole
     or Santero or some shit."
Mel pats her brow with the royal towel.
Sees Spur across the wings, urgently whispering
to his mom, who crosses herself,
And rubs her Yoruba beads. *Goddamnit, Spur.*
Echo-No-Mics echoing her son's stern look of concern.
Both glance Mel's way; her gaze locks on Spur—
now, she's the one feeling butthurt.

Meanwhile, Heavy sniffs a bump of blow
from the detachable tip of his Raw-Y'all Records Jesus piece.
Mel fears he'll stop the show when he knows
about the creature, ghost, or whatever it was.
But she sees Echo-No-Mics all up in Spur's ear,
dictating instructions, sending him off
with a wave, like: *No, just go*
as Echo returns to the judges' table in the orchestra pit,
     all boss.

Mel thanking God and all the gods—
good-golly giddy in her apprehensive bones
as Heavy wipes residual snow from his nose,
coke-fueled, oblivious to the drama,
cold, post skiing the slopes,

Mel peeping his steeze as the king says:
    "Fuck Lil Whateva-His-Name-Is."
And takes her behind the stage, like herding cattle,
faded red curtains rising and parting.
Time for battle.

ം

Truth-Is' voice on the mic:
        "Hey, y'all, we got Lil Bone-A-Part versus
        Pretty-Dope comin' up next. We servin' it up nice,
        long and hot, like sex on a platter."
Mel pivots to Heavy,
not expecting to witness him put on his stage face.
Deep breath. Like even the king still gets edgy.
She can hardly believe her shrink-wrapped Zen, born anew
when she's guided into the spotlight by the living legend.
Sacred psychedelic ceremony in the holy brightness.
Ritual like the Prophet's sponsoring her communion into the
    zeitgeist. VIP
in the making. Footfalls on air, gliding
on springs. Keys to the kingdom hers if she wants them—just
    gotta reach out
and take 'em. Already come all this way.
Initiated. Reminding Mel of when Mima was sacramented
    with Yoruba beads.
Truth-Is plays it off to the congregation like:
        "Oh, peep this. P-Dope
        gettin' a special escort
        from His Highness."
Sweet Lady Jane chimes in at the king
from the judges' table in the orchestra pit:

"Don't go gettin' me jealous, bae."
Mel beams, living the dream, even with a nightmare
underneath, still Heaven.
Heavy hands her over to Truth-Is like a dead-beat dad.
Waking her out of the moment.
Heads to his judges' table throne—leaving Mel alone
with Truth, the DJ, and the crowd (Led Zeppelin's Ocean).   200
Better not drown.

⁏

About the same time,
Lil Bone-A-Part finds
the "OUT OF SERVICE" sign hanging
on the gentlemen's door backstage.
Fuck it. Goes into the ladies'.

Water drip-drops from the ceiling
to the tiles in beat
with the LIGHT FLICKER
as Bone-A-Part enters.   210
The dread emcee *eeny-meeny-miny-moes,*
enters a stall, shuts its SQUEAKING GATE.
Lil Bone-A-Part drains the lizard
as LIGHTBULBS FLICKER.
Stall door's bolt-less,
so he keeps elbowing it
back in place—
    SQUEAK... SQUEAK... SQUEAK...
Bone-A-Part practicing:
    "Lil B in the house - y'all know me   220
    Girls, take off your blouse

'Cuz I'm so aroused, see?"
He hears the restroom DOOR
OPEN
and CLOSE.
   "When I gots to pee, it's gots
   To be – 'cuz I'm the ocean and
   Y'all drops in the sea"
He finishes up…
      DRIP, DRIP … DRIP,
            DROP…
   "Give you golden showers from ivory towers
   With Lil Bone-A-Part's lyrical powers
   Fertilize all your fuckin' flowers"
Bone-A-Part steals a bump of yey from a baggy.
Tucks it back into the waistband of his boxers,
   senses sharpening.
   "Now, we ready."
Turns away from the toilet without flushing,
opens the stall gate—
      SQUEAK—

          ✍

A NEEDLE SCRATCHES
on the turntable as the DJ SPINS FILLER.
Mel's feet TAP on the hardwood, more alarmed by
   the moment.
Sweating under the lights. Impatient silhouettes stare back.
She can make out faces in the front, unsatiated, about
   to combust.
Can't front, that ain't the only ping in her gut.

Bad mojo coming over her, as if staring at the world from 250
    beyond
a veil. An off sense, hard to dispel.
Smoothie of adrenal juices, blender about to start.
Mel whispers to Truth-Is:
        "Where's Bone-A-Part?"

Scarlet Jackson Pollock

MEL SEES TRUTH-IS look to the wings
and Nicole Echo-No-Mics signal her there's time
to buy.
Mel doesn't wanna begin to suppose why.

Truth-Is covers the mic,
says to Mel:
    "You need to do something."
        "Do somethin' like what?"
    "Ain't this what you been waiting for?
    Shake that sexy ass, lead a prayer—
    whatev. Or they'll never forgive you."
Truth turns back to the audience:

146

"Miss Dope here just volunteered
to keep us all entertained
while we wait, y'all."
Mel turns to Truth, like:
Why you adding more pressure?
Loudest voices in the pack signing up:
            "Let her rhyme!"
                "Entertain, bitch!"
                    "Here we go again with this one!"
            "Ain't no emcee!"
                "Fucking loser!"
                    "Big titty scrub!"
                        "Bay Harbor Posse, wussup!"
                "Yo, talk to your friend, dawg!"
Laughter. Yelling. Yodeling.
Peanut gallery chorus, ugly.
Mel looks to the king, hyped
for battle but out on a limb.
Her hero gives her no help,
studies her all stealth, *help yourself.*
                    Princess or jester?
Fuck letting the question fester.
Sure, no pressure. Naturally auto-tuned. No quantizing
    Pro Tools.
Some loud dude of the same mind:
            "Show us what you got, bitch!"
Mel whips in the voice's direction,
as if possessed:
    "How about you show us what you got,
    Bitch? Glitch in your head probably
    Goes to where your dick is"

Mel doesn't know where this is going,
but she rides it:
>   *"Sad song, wired wrong*
>   *I clap back with bulletproof fap facts*
>   *Bet you piss through the slits*
>   *In your nose, Rick*
>   *Now, that's just some sick shit"*   50
Mel like: *Where'd that come from?*
Takes a step back,
shocked at herself.
Like it's mystical.
From a higher power.
>   But the troll in the crowd's too conceited
>   to concede it, screaming:
>   "Bitch, get on your knees!"
>   Big dude, fulla more hot air
>   than paraphernalia.   60
Another hater calls out:
>   "You ain't all that!"
And another:
>   "Fucking wack!"
Mel like:
>   *"I ain't all that, but I ain't all wack,*
>   *No*
>   *Take what you say and rhyme-bust back,*
>   *Yo*
>   *Just fine*   70
>   *Melodic like a Paul MaC bass line,*
>   *Tho*
>   *One of a kind like the Bride of Frankenstein*
>   *Strapped tight in a Goldman Sachs breadline,*

So I go from day 'til dusk, and all the night-time,
Fo sho
Y'all better know your waterfall
Whine packs my grapevine with flows
Sublime and juicy punch lines, ho"

Backstage, Spur listens,
forgetting conferring stagehands,
moving closer to the wings.
Pretty-Dope's voice over the speakers
spitting lines like:
    "Rock your bells, bells, bells,
    Bells, bells, like Poe and LL…"
Spur grins despite himself.

Onstage, Mel like:
    "Mama and the Raven said, 'knock you out,' so
    Someone tell the ref to ring the fuckin' bell, bell, bell"
People getting into it—heads nodding,
clapping, WHISTLING.
Mel peacocks for Heavy and the judges.
How you like that?
Heavy nods, intrigued.

Nicole Echo-No-Mics takes her seat
at the judges' table, sees
Heavy, her brother Bettino, watching Pretty-Dope
with bling signs in his eyes.
Nicole leans close, speaks
with her hand over her judge's microphone:
        "She's mala suerte, bro.

Watching out for you.
Feel me?"
No response. Nicole follows up:
"I ain't no gif, meme or emoji—
don't goddamn ignore me."
"Got a little Janelle Monáe to her,
don't she? Petite, quirky and funky."
Before Nicole can respond, Bettino taps his wrist like a watch.   110
"What's-His-Name musta fell in.
Have Spur fetch the lil fuck."

Seconds late, Spur pushes through
the entrance to the backstage ladies lavatory.
Scans the stalls,
checks under them all
for shoes. Finds none.
He pushes each door open. Empty,
echoing down the row.
Reaches the end, about to call it: 120
No luck, lil dude's gone home.
Growing relieved that there's nothing to see
as he opens the last stall, finds
a splash of blood on the wall
above the toilet—
like a scarlet Jackson Pollock.
No sign of Bone-A-Part.

Onstage, Mel battles back remaining hecklers,
haters, shouting out shit like:

> "Fuck you, lil bitch!   130
>   Go watch My Little Pony!"
Mel flinging and slinging it, clapping back:
> *"Fuck me?*
> *Dude, I need a dude with a dick that ain't a brittle phony*
> *Homie compensating being rude"*

The groundlings dig it.
King Heavy studies Pretty-Dope
like he must've been studied himself.
Almost appears jealous of the mob's love.
Nicole Echo-No-Mics looking like she wants to call it a forfeit,   140
the king looking like he wants to hear none of it.
Mel holds sway, swinging at verbal pitches—
voice in the crowd calling out:
>   "Where you from?"
Mel like:
> *"Central Florida trailer park slums, burnt toast, egg crumbs*
> *Hence, torrid events led to Mom's bums, who stare for awhile*
> *Like at art, and torment beds like farts*
> *While Mima frets about hair, gums, sexy selfies to post,*
> *And Art, and Greg the Sequel*   150
> *Looking back through a looking-glass peephole*
> *Peek-whole, good people:*
> *Not going back, rather be dead*
> *Pretty ending this sum of parts*
> *Staring at stars like I'm equal—"*
She dodges out of Heavy's way—
the king springing from the table, back to the stage
in a blur—he barrels into the spotlight
and takes the mic from her, like:

"Now that's a hungry-sounding
        emcee. Y'all feel me?"
The CROWD CHEERS.

Sees Heavy reach into the wings,
pull the first emcee he sees: Kandela Del Fuego.
The king goes on:
        "Alright, we done with the warm up.
        Got a cat fight on the mic."
Mel's cups the mic, whispers to Heavy:
    "Where's Bone-A-Part?"
Heavy says:
        "We finna switch out emcees."
Mel's eyes drift to the wings,
where V@$T @ppe@l and his crew leave like: *WTF?!*
Meanwhile, Kandela leans to the mic in Heavy's hand:
        "Del Fuego on deck."
She points at Mel:
        "Ayo, ayo—fuck this bitch, yo!"
Mel forces a smile like she's unfazed. Does a royal wave.
Kandela like:
        "I electroshock hoes that ain't
        Hot shit, bro, so—"
Heavy like:
        "Okay, save it—
        let's get these bitches on the clock."
Mel's eyes drift back to the wings.
What the hell happened to Lil B?

Heavy like:
    "Roll it, Truth."

Mel returns her focus
when Truth-Is taps a tab on her phone.										190
And the electric clocks start
to COUNT DOWN from 45…
Kandela grabs the mic stand like a rocker:
>*"One of a kind?*
>*Careful, like Sondheim, bitch*
>*Get back in line*
>*Hammerstein gonna hammer your self-esteem*
>*It's Hammer Time, ain't no stammering lines*
>*No blabbering vibes, no chattering mimes—*
>*Just shattering shrines with staggering rhymes*										200
>*Time you knew you ain't nothin' new, boo*
>*Goddaughter 'bout to get baptized in bong water"*

Catches Mel off-guard with her opening shot.
The CROWD "OHHS" and "AHHS" already.
Kandela points at Miles in the holstered water bottle at
   Mel's side:
>*"Gonna leave your goldfish alone*
>*Since your backpack be the only home it knows"*

Mel opens her arms like *have at it.*
But her confidence leaks a little										210
with every Kandela line:
>*"Tonight, you drop a rhyme from*
>*The heart*
>*Rap 'bout trailer park slums*
>*and guys named Art*
>*But you ain't love the art*
>*You just wanna be a star*
>*Drop your draws*
>*Just to bag a start*

Trash-chute fast   220
Just to land a part"
Mel, on the ropes,
grins and bears the verbal assault,
no other choice but play it off.
Kandela like:
    "Duped unwisely
    Psyched by shit shiny
    Jewel-seduced jit
    Juiced for salvation, salivatin'
    Kudos, props, money, adulation   230
    I ain't hatin'—just Sixth-Sensin'
    Pretty-Dope's destination"
The HERD HOOTS and HOLLERS
and Mel struggles to process
the information. Spotlight hot,
as the sun gets. Bad invocation.
Her time melting like in a Salvador Dali painting.
Feeling the flock turn against her.
Defeat welling in her eyes
as Kandela goes for the prize: 240
    "Craven, craving ovations, shakin'
    Losing it waitin', impatient
    Talkin' to ravens
    Gettin' they pity be shitty
    Sayin' you ain't never
    Makin' it in the city, state,
    Or nation
    Dyin' of starvation
    Struggle lost in the jungle
    The desert, the woods"   250

Kandela's FACE REPLACED with faces
from Mel's past in Kandela's place—
LIP-SINGING RHYMES:
Mima,
Art the Prequel,
Greg the Sequel,
and kids from school back in the day
—Mel a LITTLE GIRL again…
…remembering…
Thou Who Shall Remain Nameless.   260
Even her day one, Rosa, up in the mix.
The ugly truth of her youth:
Alone with Mima, no don dada to call her own, just another
        jit from a broken home.
Idlewild like a Bryan Barber cinematic tome. Someone get
        Abuelita on the phone.
Rollin' stone without a papa musta been a beast of burden.
Always moving, perpetual outsider
at school. Kids cruel. Mel uncool:
the one who wasn't invited   270
to birthday parties and got left out,
except when it came to getting taunted
and turnt out. Turned off. Torn down. Beat and burned out.
How she'd wanted to escape,
sink into the stage like ink on a page—
paper like sheets to hide beneath,
sniffling in her pjs.
Scheherazade.
A thousand and one days and nights. At least.
Glenn Miller serenade by the moonlight.   280
Backpack full of secondhand dolls and dad's cassette tapes.

An eclectic collection of tunes, all the fucker-of-mothers
    had left;
Mima called it a bunch of shit,
but for Mel, the recordings raised her—
until Mima had to sell the stash to put fast food on the table.
Oh, how Mel wanted to do her own thing, show them all she
    was worth her weight.
Dreamed she could be a rapper, famous as a singer.
Or a super-producer, a proven winner.
How she wished she had a bass, callous her own fingers.
Make beats from micro-chopped samples and live instruments
in the basement, baking donuts like Dilla.
Heaven-sent sweet scent, bakery-appealing.
Icing on the pastry, sure as "Bob" means "Marley" or "Dylan."
Have nice pearls and curls,
beloved like a diva.
Piano lessons and fancy dresses.
Traditional avenues to achieving acceptance.
Or at least accessories.
Butterscotch pudding after school and hop scotch, hip stuff.
Hair and sound like Esmeralda Spaulding's.
And Sunday nights at Families R Us.
How she'd just wanted to be…
                        enough.
Now, Kandela's humbling her, telling her she's not.
Ugly truth of her youth giving way
to the fuggly truth of her adulthood.
Realizing there's no escape.
Observing Kandela like she's an older version of Mel herself,
who's been through worse. And is better. Del Fuego like:
            "Fool kid,

> *Casket lid droppin'*
> *Like a white towel in a boxin' ring floppin'*
> *'Cuz you*
> *Lost the you*
> *In you"*

Mel back to her ADULT SELF, pummeled
by the rhymes as time expires.
Glances at Heavy, sees him waiting
for her reply. Clock reset.
Distressed, she looks around,
spots Truth-Is' mic.
Grabs it, Mel
stitching a response:
> *"Yeah, Kandela wanna talk 'bout playin' parts*
> *Even though she dyes her hair with a red shock*
> *And imitates the role of ghetto-goth bitch like a*
> *Broadway star*
> *Even the sightless seeing*
> *She compensating, comping Satan*
> *Consternating but… but she, uh—"*
Drowned out by the LOUD CROWD BOOING,
as if underwater.
Yemayá, Goddess of the Sea, washing over her.
But who's watching over her?
Under the Valdemar canopy, trying to call on Calliope.
Cadence clipped. Seeking balance in the badlands,
like a raven on a bust of Pallas Athena—
with wings snipped.
Scatter brain reined in, battered.
Rhyme taken out of her,

lines not occurring
in her mind,
nouns and verbs
in a bind, not lining up.
Altering her time signature,
overriding her clock,
turned over like a misfortune card.
Seeing herself   350
an apostle Last Supper-shunned by the upper echelon.
Vagabond. Outclassed.
Kandela lowers her mic to rejoice
in the flock's reaction. Sticks
out her tongue ring
with the grinning skull stud.
PING! POW!—what it feels like now.

Pity Pretty-Dope, unworthy of a Pietà.

Mel lowers her mic to her side,
squeezing it,   360
all she has left, struggling
to play it cool, exposed as a fake.
Kandela like:
   "So let's nip this scrub shrub in the bud
    Before she bloom into a dud"
Kandela raises her mic to her lips, and—
a white-hot arc of HIGH-PITCHED ELECTRICITY
  sends volts
vibrating through her—
    ZAP!—ZAP!—ZAP!—   370
sparks of Jacob's arc, sizzling,

grilling her raw.
FEEDBACK SINGING OFF-KEY,
frequencies zigging and zagging,
vocal pitch hopping up the scale from contralto to soprano,
fulla zing in the swing, Kandela's body shaking,
hair frying, nerves fraying, mic smoking, skin toking, roasting.
Emcee skewer,
smelling like microwave chicken and a flame hitting
    weed resin.
Wide eyes juiced with surprise,
begging: *Kill me!*
Mel has to turn away, glances up
to the catwalk,
finds some *thing* in the shadows peering down;
red orb eyes are all she sees, locked in her sight.
Mel, startled, drops
her mic—it SHRIEKS FEEDBACK.
She hears
Nicole Echo-No-Mics bark at stagehands:
       "Kill the lights! Pull the curtain!"
Lights go off
and Kandela drops
at Mel's stunned feet, who looks back up, and sees the red orbs
    are gone.
What. The. Fuck.
Glances back at the body,
smoking death mask in stingy light—
AC traces in footlight filaments fading—
when she's jolted by Heavy
raising her hand, saying:
    "Give it the fuck up for the winner

of this battle:
Pretty-Dope!"
Guiding everyone's attention away
from the body.
    "Those sure was some fly FX,
    but we goin' by rhymes here,
    and only one can move on.
    Now, give it up one more time
    for mutha-fucking Pretty-Dope!"
Through the blur and shock, Mel
makes out the subjects following
their king, mirroring his words
for all their worth:
        "Mutha-fucking Pretty-Dope!"
            "Mutha-fucking Pretty-Dope!"
                "Mutha-fucking Pretty-Dope!"
Mel's too discombobulated to bask in the moment.
Heavy like:
    "DJ, drop another beat!"
DJ Turtleman obliges, CUTS ANOTHER RECORD.
The CURTAIN CLOSES.

Feedback (Skit)

DEAD EYES WIDE,
   staring back
    bare facts,
accusatory, the story they tell:
On you, Mel. Prolly going to Hell.

Mel turns to Heavy,
who drops her hand backstage
as the curtain splits them
from the audience.
DJ's dropped record spinning a distraction,
Heavy's classic gem, "Manifest the Best."
Surreal for Mel to hear it while the king himself studies her,
suspicious but drawn to her as well.
She speaks low:

"I don't got nothing to do with this."
  "Don't care if ya did."
Not even looking at her when he says it.
Heavy calls out to the gathering crowd, covering
their view with a gold and white-gold smile:
  "She's all good, homies.
    Just got the wind knocked outta her.
    Finna be more than fine."

He orders security to clear the backstage crush—
contestants, techs, and stagehands, at bay—
even the Cuban chaperones—
leaving the group guarded like Guantanamo.
Kandela apparently had no entourage to speak of.
Only those standing close know something's wrong.
Truth-Is, a witness, collapsing from the sight,
influencer suffering entropy,
arms wrapped around her knees, shivering.
Dudes trying to help, cop feels for themselves.
Security making them disperse.
Sweet Lady Jane on the other side, seeming pissed
at what's become of her. Empathy leaking.

Mel turns back to Kandela's remains,
heat steaming off her face.
Kneels to the body, reaches out...
When Spur WHACKS the mic
from Kandela's grip with a broomstick.
        "Still live."
Mel pulls back,
feeling the burning on the tips of her fingers,

she hears a loud SLAM—
spins, tense—
sees Echo-No-Mics by a fuse box,
crossing herself.

> "Some *thing*
> fucked with this
> electrical shit." 50

Spur like:

> "Lifted the ground on the gear."

Heavy like:

"Somebody. Not some *thing*."
Spur says:

> "Some *thing*. We saw it down low."

Echo-No-Mics starts to pray, the full Mojuba,
calling on all ancestors and gods
as Mel feels Heavy's gaze sharpen on her.
Spur drops another bombshell, this one on Mel: 60

> "And Bone-A-Part's missing.
> All that's left's a bunch of blood.
> Thing we saw must've done all this."

Mel struck by shrapnel from
the part 'bout Lil Bone-A-Part,
the dread bred to be a star.

Doesn't wanna believe it. But she's seen
some of it with her own eyes. Horrified.
Tragedies multiplied. Guilt respites forbidden.
Not what she had in mind for the climb. 70
Can't take her eyes off Kandela's body,
victim number three. Says:

> "Not like this."

Heavy not listening,
too distracted dealing with shit.
Speaking low to Spur, within Mel's earshot:
    "Dump it where you dumped the other."
Mel's more than disturbed, more than unnerved.
Sees Spur's urgent protest but doesn't hear the words.
Echo-No-Mics interjecting, debate in the inner circle,
excluding Mel.
Anyway, Heavy gets his way. Nothing more to say.
Kandela's body 'bout to be moved like a prop,
Spur keeps saying to Heavy:
                "We gotta stop the show."
        "Not now. Go."
                "Bro—"
    "Ain't gonna say it again, College."
Mel stops the parade. Slips off her hoodie,
covers Kandela's face, wide dead eyes.
But Heavy snatches it off and tosses it back.
    "You slow?"
Mel sees the body disappear down a corridor.
Spur a pallbearer, glancing back
as Mel turns to Heavy, who eyes her cautiously
while telling Sweet Lady Jane:
    "Get out there. Keep shit moving."
Jane sniffles, wipes tears from lashes:
                "Sayin' what, bae?
                I ain't co-judge for whatever
                this shit is to go down like this, H.
                Oh, my Lord.
                You promised no more drama."
    "Desperate times. Want back in

the spotlight? Get the fuck out there
and ease the people, Jane.
    Don't make me ask again."
Mel scoping for an opening:
        "H, listen—"
Heavy turns to Echo-No-Mics rubbing her beads:
    "Get more bouncers back here."
Mel trying to show him she's serious,
seriously needs to talk.
        "Your Highness."
But Heavy's saving her for last, watching
the orders put into action… show re-starting
on the far side of the curtain…
Sweet Lady Jane's voice coming through:
                "Uh… Kandela's gonna be alright, y'all.
                So, uh, the big Q is… are y'all ready
                for some more?!"

                    ᦂ

Mel follows Heavy through the backstage, king drawing
    his Glock,
in damage control, down a corridor—kicking open doors,
finding nothing. Mel like:
        "I know the optics ain't good—
        she was kickin' my ass,
        but I was gonna come back.
        She died before I could slay her.
        I only kill with words."
Still nothing as Heavy checks another door—
        "Now."
And another door—when she stops him:

"Bettino White.
Do I need to grab
a hot fuckin' mic
for you to listen?"
Double-gets his attention.
    "Don't you dare fuckin' play
with me like that."   140
She exhales sixteen bars in the confession booth:
        "Spur was spilling the truth.
    There's
    some
    thing
    here.
    I seen it. Down in the bowels
    and, I think, again right just now."
"You seen a rat. That's that."
        "We gotta end the show.   150
    It ain't safe."
"Gonna sacrifice your shot?"
        "You seen what I can do,
    and I got a demo I can give you
    to listen to if you got any doubts,
    but it's time to depart, ride out,
    lights out, detour to 95 South.
    Or North—whatever—or both."
    "Nah. Two more rounds to go."
H takes a bump from his Raw-Y'all Jesus piece.   160
In the harsher light, she sees
the yellow gold under the rhodium
of all his bling, wear and tear, time unfair.
She says to him:

"King, c'mon!"

V@$T @ppe@l surges up out of nowhere
with what's left of his crew, corners Mel:
      "Blood all over the bathroom,
      fucking black cat cunt!
      What you up to, bitch?"
Mel scans past him. Bone-A-Part's absence
conspicuous. Bracing to see his ghost.
She looks to Heavy, but he's still trying to decipher
her soul. Big hand wrapped around his Glock.
Judge and executioner, like: *you're still on your own.*
Meanwhile, V@$T @ppe@l like:
      "Who you working with?"
All eyes on Mel—suspicious, venomous.
      "I ain't workin' with nobody. Han Solo
      in this whole shit. And I ain't got nothin'
      to do with—"
      "Errbody in your way keeps dropping,
      but you don't know shit."
Scared and isolated,
Mel's ready to dispel the myth he's coming with:
      "I'm about to explode
      like a dream deferred
      if you don't back up
      and cut that wack snuff.
      All I know is a fuckin' ghost
      or monster
      or some *thing*.
      Almost scratched me off.
      That's whose face you need to be foggin'."

V@$T @ppe@l scoffs:
>   "Monster?"
Heavy bitch-slaps V@$T, surprising everyone.
>   "Next round. You up."
Heavy holsters his gun, turns to Mel:
>   "Go wash. Meditate. Medicate. Masturbate.
>   And be ready, 'cuz you still in this."
Heavy back to directing emergency traffic.
Pretty-Dope acting tough as she goes, frustrated
with herself, putting up a front:
>   "Splash, splash—like new.
>   Here's a preview:
>   *V@$T @ppe@l, name says it all*
>   *Style over substance, doomed to subsist*
>   *Can't ignite a crowd with your sound not profound*
>   *Ball-bound, no way to make 'em go Wild Child*
>   *Ain't you seen 8 Mile, Child?"*
She flips styles to sample his:
>   *"Flickin' my whip, whip, whip, flickin' my, flickin' my*
>   *whip, whip, whip*
She keeps walking—V@$T being led the other way,
rubbing his cheek, baritone barking:
>   "Dawg! Fuck!
>   She guilty!
>   Gonna fuck you up, bitch!"
As Mel turns a corner, audiophile, the tough front she's tried
    to hold gives,
guilt weighing on her shoulders.

❧

Seventy-three seconds later, alone in the corridor by the
    back exit,
Mel wipes tears and snot from her face with her sleeve.
Sees the gentlemen's with the "OUT OF ORDER" sign;
ladies' where Bone-A-Part performed a disappearance,
    Houdini-style.
She realizes she's alone…
Wonders where all the good ghosts and gods are right now,
when she needs them most. Something inside telling her: *this
    is about me.*
Telling people it ain't, but what else could it be?
Black cat, witchcraft, Angel of Doom.
She reaches for the restroom, when her eyes catch a
    FLICKERING "EXIT" sign—
stage door—by a dust-covered admin desk, clock-in/
    out machine.
She looks back at the dried blood on her hands.
What else is you supposed to do?
So tempting to give in, the gig up—
whatever it is, irrelevant, part of a greater plan, Mel a pawn,
carbon-based lifeform in the cold, indifferent vastness of space.
Something supernatural playing her like a piece.
Not sure what to believe anymore, except:

Not your day. Not your decade.
Not your lifetime, alternate reality, or nirvana.
Stop fighting fate, against signs from the stars.
Shit be so hard: fall down, get up, fall down,
struggle to stand, fall, ground coming toward—
obstacles, weights, headwinds,
barely off the ground, fall down.

Wanna get up again now?
Catch a beat down.
What once could be touched, abstract,
intangible. Tired of shit, easier to Netflix on the couch
and eat a sandwich.
Why not just let it go?
How bad would that be?
Forget Bono saying, "You only lose when you quit."   260
Embrace dreams of leaving a legacy dying.
Get it over with.
Can almost feel the weight lift off her essence,
beyond the heft of boulders, bolder to shoulder
the burden no longer.
Just stop trying…
         Trying to thrive against the tide…
                  Tide pushing upstream in a tsunami.
The true test:
when it hurts from soul to spine,   270
and you keep on going—
despite divine neglect—
and they still egg you on: "Just prove it."
Heart on your sleeve, leave you an amputee—
if some thing doesn't get you first, end your thirst.

'Bout to float this bail, she lets go
of the restroom door. Stalks
toward the stage door,
below the FLICKERING "EXIT."
Clenching fists in fear   280
and frustration.
Each step of her Adidas

killing a little more of her vision board.
Fighting back tears, she reaches
the exit—
but stops.
Hearing Heavy's voice in real life like:
    "Whoa, whoa, whoa—slow your roll."
Heavy catching up, like:
    "Forget that shit. Just be happy
    you movin' to the next round. We
    finna deal with the rest after."
Mel peeks back at the path to the stage,
then back at the exit.
Wipes a fat tear off her cheek fast as she can.
Heavy like:
    "You said you wanna be like me.
    Shit be hard sometimes.
    Just how it is."
        "But not like this."
She pushes open the door—Heavy like:
    "I know your life.
    Where you think I come from?
    Seven-One, right…
    but there ain't nothin' else about my hist.
    Not from before Bettino White started ballin'.'"
Mel watches Heavy produce a BULGING MONEY-CLIP
with a crown on it. He snaps out a wad of bills, counts:
    "Old boy nowhere to be found.
    Old girl fulla more chemicals than a pharmacy.
    Bringin' a new… to our room every night—
    kickin' us out, makin' us wait
    by the fuckin' dirty motel pool."

Mel watching him count bills the whole time.
     "My sis and me belly achin', tryin' to stretch
     three meals outta a microwaved pie
     of Mama Celeste and a past-due milk."
          "You never put that in' your rhymes."
     "Unlike every other fool, right?
     They could keep that shit. I wanted to forget.
     Create my own persona."
          "Why you Deep-Throating me this?"
     "Because I escaped it. But you finna
     go back. Next step, sellin' ass."
He extends a hand full of cash.
She holds the door, wary. Eyes him like he's trying to buy
     her soul.
Stares up at the king. Conflicted.
     "Leave or stay, it's yours. Take it," he says.
Just a few hundred, but it's more
than she's used to seeing. Contest entry fee plus interest.
     "Want crypto instead?"
She takes a deep breath, and shuts the door—
still inside. Heavy like:
     "Now, back to biz.
     You up in a few ticks."

Mel reaches for the stack.
Heavy closes her hands around the bills.
     "Finna thank me when you win this, Pretty-Dope."
          "Pretty-Dope's the alias.
          My real name's Melody."
     "Well, shit, Mellow-Dee.
     With a name like that, we

ain't even need another."
And with that, Heavy heads back to the show; Mel watches
    him go.
She takes one last glance at the exit stage door, pockets
    the cash.

Pretty-Dope's Destination

(Interlude)

CREEPED OUT TO be alone, Mel steps into the ladies' backstage, on alert.

QUAD ECHOING from the distant proscenium.
Too far away. Still afraid.
Fluorescent LIGHTS FLICKER.
WATER DRIPS from rusty pipes.
Stalls parallel to sink basins, missing mirrors
except the one at the far end.
A row of closed doors. She crouches, scans the stalls.

Nothing but porcelain mantles. Mel moves fast, past them all   10
to get to the mirror, WHISTLING "Killa,"
in a half-baked attempt to calm her nerves.
Splashes water on her face, alone in FLICKERING
LIGHT. Peeks behind her reflection…
just in case. All clear, thank gods.
She taps a soap dispenser.
Empty.
So she scrubs her hands harder,
struggling to rinse off dried specks of gore.

In her REFLECTION: a CROWN APPEARS,   20
Basquiat-style,
more imagination graffiti.
Mel raps Kandela's disses at herself,
haunted by the words:
    "Jewel-seduced jit juiced for
    salvation, salivatin' kudos, props,
    money, adulation -
    just Sixth-Sensin' Pretty-Dope's destination"
The crown above her reflection replaced by graffiti
    DEVIL HORNS.   30
Then the HORNS get ~~CROSSED OUT~~
~~along with her face.~~
    Artist fed up with a sketch.
It all disappears.
Mel alone, like Cudi on the Moon,
with nothing but herself staring back…
CREAK-BAM!
Something SLAMS in a stall behind her—
she spins with a start—

finds nothing but the path back to the closed restroom door,   40
flanked by the row of stalls.
The one closest to the exit swaying slightly
on a fractured hinge, tapping the frame…
FAINTER and fainter…

         TAP…   TAp…   Tap…

Someone here?

      …tap…

Like a flame she can't help touch, she begins checking stalls.
Finds nothing
but dick drawings and old tags.   50
Pushes another door. Then another.
Getting closer to the final stall with the slanted gate…

         …tap…

Buying time with the other stalls,
prolonging the inevitable.

        …tap…

She reaches the final stall.
Her fingers reach toward the door
on the slanted hinge…
Here goes…   60

She pushes it open…
Finds a scarlet fresco coagulating to brown.
The last remains of Bone-A-Part's physical graffiti.
Where he must have disappeared.
She spots a broken hinge on the floor.
Where it must have come loose. Disturbed,
Mel still exhales, relieved she's alone.
A KNOCK at the door startles her, followed by:

"Yo,
        she-who-wants-to-end-
        up-like-the-girl-in-a-Poe-story,
        H says you're up in five."
It's just Spur. Thank the gods he's made it back from
    the depths.
Not about to let him know she's relieved:
    "On my way."
She looks back at Bone-A-Part's blood on the wall.
Spur knocks again, voice coming through:
        "Guess it didn't work out
        with getting H to stop the show."
    "He's the king, right?
    What was I supposed to do?"
Genuinely wants to know.
On the DL, she hopes
there's still a chance for something
between them. Something decent.
He finally answers:
        "Let's get out of here."

Seeming to read her pause, he goes on:
        "We'll come up with a plan once we're safe.
        I've met some folks. I can always make a few calls.
        Nothing owed. We don't gotta fuck—
        unless you want to—separate matter, altogether.
        Point is, no strings. Favor's free of cost.
        Lives have been lost. You want on that list?
        There are other options. That's all I'm trying to say."
Why can't she embrace it? Is his premise so crazy?
Questions about the person she is, persistent.

"I can't quit."
        Her voice lets it slip out.   100
No peppering the void with petty quotes.
Guilt and shame playing games with Pretty-Dope.
She listens to Spur take a deep breath, sigh cutting
through barricades. It precedes his apparent conceding.
Mel feeling the feelings fleeing,
instrumental interlude fading,
gone like a breeze over a shimmering bay of lights,
hearing Spur say:
        "Wish I never saw that Poe book,
        or gave you that dough.   110
        What the hell you even thinking, sticking
        around after all this shit for? Know what, forget it.
        That's for you to figure out."
    "I said, on my way—"
WHAM!
Something comes right at her—
she jumps back.
Sees the slanted stall door CRASH
to the floor—its final hinge landing beside it.
Just a chicken, that's what she is.   120
She kicks the hinge—sick of this shit.
And sick of being sick of it and other things.

Spur knocks again, like:
        "What was that? You okay?"
Mel responds with:
    "'Straight ballin'
    like Tupac collaborating
    with Thug Life..."

"Then hurry up.
Before there's any more drama." 130
BAM—she hears Spur KICK the door.
The sound rips her attention
away from the bloody wall
to the exit/entrance.
Moods swinging, not looking good
for those DL hopes of a romantic reunion.
Okay, asshole.
She steps toward the door, when
the LIGHTS FLICKER and SHUT OFF.
Mel freezes. 140
"Stop fuckin' around, Spur."
KNOCK, KNOCK, KNOCK. She sparks her phone's light.
"Ding, ding, ding. I get it."
Makes her way to the door as the KNOCKING
CONTINUES.
Finds the handle:
"Don't be a dick."
She opens the door.
Where's Spur?
Facedown on the floor. 150
"Oh, fuck a shit…"
She reaches down, out into the hall—
"No, no, no…"
—but finds him barely conscious, thanks gods.
Glances around, when—
Spur stirs. Concussed. Looks behind her—
into the restroom.
Retinas wide, like they retain ghosts.
She turns toward the stalls—

LIGHTS FLICKER ON—

Mel sees her shadow on a wall.

LIGHTS FLICKER OFF.

Lost in darkness.

LIGHTS FLICKER BACK ON—and now

a

LARGE

SHADOW'S

on the wall

behind

hers—

Oh, gods—

She spins, right into a wall,

a bulwark, an obstacle—

except it's not a wall at all—it has arms—THEY

ENVELOP HER.

LIGHTS FLICKER DARK AGAIN.

Mel SCREAMS—deep from the source—until she's hoarse.

It's useless. All for naught. She's fucked.

Track 16

Underground Remix

WHEN HER EYES focus again, dazed,
the first thing Mel sees is the discreet light
of random candles, melting wax
like glue onto the concrete foundation,
covered in roaches—
and not the good kind smokers savor;
belly-up creepy crawlies.
Supposed to survive nuclear holocausts—
but not this nest. *Where is this?*

Scavenged possessions. Stereo with speakers
that don't match. Walls lined with STACKED
NOTEBOOKS, note pads, napkins.

10

Parchment and velum hosting mold, mildew.
Smells like sewage and puke.
A lair where a creature's dwelled a long time.
On the lowest level of the theater, must be.
Shit.
Water dripping onto her face
from the ceiling. Taste the rotten liquid
mix with the salt of her sweat and iron and lead
from a busted lip. Then she sees…
The some *thing.*
A man
with a RIPPED,
ragged SHIRT wrapped across his face
like a gang-banger's mask. Or some ninja shit.

He drags her—struggling and shrieking—to the stereo. Slaps
headphones on her. *Fuck!* Scared to death
of ending up like 1DaFull—as the monster
holds her up. Presses play—Mel like:
    "No!"
Headphones pinned to her head. She resists,
but it's no use. The song plays
and Mel braces herself—
but the volume doesn't blow her eardrums.
Blows her mind instead; a familiar voice like:
    "Sick of the sidelines, I gotta get mine
    Shine - divine mind for our times, my advice
    To the gentlemen, ladies, and babies
    Be an emcee killa
    Before an emcee kill ya
    Do you in for a label

That can't feel or see ya
Kill an emcee where it hurts,
Soft underbelly in the megahertz
Beat a drum with hooks and bars
Stab a song in the back, no love"

Memories rush up like stickup kids
ready to jack her for all she's got.
Like a music video, **FLASHBACK TO**   50
INT. A CRAMPED MIAMI APARTMENT - NIGHT
 (1999)
Young Melody, no older than six,
playing with an MPC beat machine. Her father's hand
over hers, adding accents to a track.
From their matching headphones, "Killa"
PLAYS,
UNFINISHED.
Already a masterpiece to her, hearing her father's voice
because it means he's home.   60
   "Killa born and reborn an orphan
   Dying to pull good from bad
   Like a rabbit from a trap, top hat, or a coffin
   Emcee dreams be all a killa ever had
   Writing rhymes since I started coughin'
   Lying for a rhyme scheme, truth be no later than
     age nine
   Now equipped with rhymes for all times
   And All Time
   —All kinds—   70
   'Cuz it's my time
   My time

My time
  To design, build and fill shrines"
Her mom, Angel Z, frets bills at the kitchen table
while Abuelita, rest in peace, cooks arroz con pollo,
steam rising, smells singing salsa, mambo and guaguancó;
kinfolk sometimes crooning along to Cole Porter:
    "Anything Goes,"
"Love for Sale"—the Great American Songbook, music of
    all sorts.

        "Hunt an emcee's verse
        Kill the chorus,
        Put it in a hearse, dispersed
        Blow up the bridge it's crossing,
        Crossing signals, drown it in an ocean,
        Mouths open, singing along, crescendo crushing 'em
           in a song
        Strangling on a mic cord, chord change they
           can't afford,
        Vocal cords collapsing, shouldn't have gone for
           that note
        But on another…
        Repeat, do it again for an outro
        Terminate the jam, the joint, the world,
        Wanna get something nice for my girls
        I'm out, y'all
        (All coda, ice cold)
        'Cuz I'm an emcee killa,
        I'm an emcee killa
        Ain't none reala - ain't none illa
        I'm an emcee killa"
Her father removes Young Mel's headphones, says:

"What you think, Melly-Mel?"
Young Mel like:
    "I'm an emcee killa, emcee killa…"
Her father, gently reaches tattooed fingers
toward her nose…
The old trick, *"I got your—"*

Mel snaps back as the monster's tattooed fingers close
around her nose…
What the fuck is happening?
Unable to gather a notion.
Frozen in shock and fear, watching it happen
like it's to someone else…
The hand pulls away from her nose,
a rough and scarred thumb between the fingers,
playing the role…
The same trick.
She shoots up off the ground—
headphone cables unplug—SOUND FILLS THE CAVE:
Her daddy's voice, altering the atmosphere:
        "Executioner emcee, serious as a samurai soldier
        Apocalypse from an esophagus, assassinate a line
        Told ya"
Mel shell-shocked, unable to speak.
She peers into the monster's eyes.
Can it be?

Track 17

Shame

"WHO ARE YOU?"

He turns away, ashamed.
A chance to run. *Now!*
But she
takes a step closer…
    Then another…
        Deep breath, and…
            Snatches his mask off—
The monster spins toward her
on instinct, fighting back fury.
Horrified, she sees…
Her dad.
Mangled face.
Mad, wounded eyes.

Red orbs bloodshot, ripped up.
Infected,
caked with pus on the edges.

Dad's alive?

Mind rolling back the tape like a time-space rewind,
remembering her daddy's face when she was a kid—
reaching out, touching the scruff on his chin,
recalling how he paused work on a song
to smile down at her, his daughter.
She reaches,
and touches his charred and scarred face—
but he flinches. Savage.
Maybe it's too late to redeem what's left.

Do I have to do this?
          Yes.
She tries again… gently.
Leaving sooted fingerprints on his sandpaper skin,
what once was scruff on his chin, now a mound of matted fur.
The monster's eyes well up, matching
her own. A tear runs
down to her fingertip.
Daddy's alive! Despite her horror, she embraces him.

The monster wraps its scarred,
tattooed-muscle arms around her,
hugs her back.
Something she thought would have to wait
for the afterlife.

She hears him WAIL a GROAN
seventeen years in the making,
feels herself let out one of her own.

In the monster's embrace, she struggles to process.
Not the monster—her dad.
Reuniting after all the years and tears, a new dawn,
red-rose fingers of the sun in the candle flames,
affection still strong, immediate connection.   50
Can almost whiff that old dad smell.
The cost of close contact: a hint of what she once had and lost.
Her lips quivering, babbling, syllables soft:
    "All this time,
    I was always rhyming
    for you."
Sensing the monster overwhelmed
by the affection, squeezing her tighter,
she lets the words go without control:
    "So that if you were still out there, you'd hear…   60
    or your ghost… or somethin'…
    I'm so, so, so, sorry—
    I just didn't want you to hate me.
    Thought that's why you left."
The monster GROANS.
It breaks what's left of her heart.
She has to know:
    "What happened?"
The monster pulls away, seeming ashamed.
Shaking his head, as much animal as human.   70
She spots a poster of Heavy on a wall. A knife
through his chest. A bitter shrine of tapes,

CDs and magazines below. Slashed.
She jolts back.
Mel stares at it, DISTANT WAILS ECHOING
in her head…

As she remembers the sound of her young WAILS,
clutching her father's MPC beat machine.
Her Abuelita trying to comfort her
as Mel looked to the front door, her Mima
speaking with an unseen man:
    "Someone has to know where he is."
Mel only glimpsed, heard fragments—but it's all coming back
now—total recall—
can almost certify him in the space
between her mom and the doorframe,
identify a thick stack of cash
and hear that familiar voice:
    "Bad dudes.
    You know he had mad enemies."
Through the crack in the door, Mel sees
the king now:
    "Could come for you next."
Heavy wiping away sweat,
urgently offering her mom a mound of bread.
Like she's back there in the room, no past tense—
straight present, one and the same—dusty needle
running on the quantum LP of time—going insane,
Cypress Hill stress on her brain witnesses Mima take
    the moolah,
and start crying, so Mel cries harder—

❧

Back in the lair
she stares at the poster of Heavy, her hero—
then her father, the monster.
She rewinds back to earlier tonight, when Bettino White
     was like:
          "That freestyle you dropped,
          where'd you get it from?"
Putting it all together in her head.
When Heavy said: 110
          "Think you know me… No clue
          what I had to do to get here…"
An illness of truth, Mel catching it,
like an influenza:
     "Oh, my God…"
Her hand squeezes into a fist
around the mask she pulled off.
The monster raises a scarred finger to her lips. *Shhh.*
A soft shush, just like when she was a kid.
Mel rejoicing to hear it again, with a brewing rage: 120
Look what they done did to my dad—
"Bad dudes," the words Heavy used when he lied to her mom,
bribed her to play dumb, as young Mel looked on.
When it was the king all along.
Abomination. Devastation. Dehumanization. Fuck.
How rotten deep is Heavy, and how deep rotten is he willing
     to go?
He did *this* to her father.
     He did *this* to *her* father.
          He did this to her father.   130

And he did *this* to *her mother.*

And he did *this* to *her.*

Robbed Mel of her saint; tender age didn't keep her safe.
Left alone with Mima, on the move, gypsy vagabonds,
cursing their losses.
Stripped of her faith that life was fair.
Sorry, kid, tragic irony is all you get.
Butterfly effect, a spider's web—
Mel flashes back to Greg
locking them in the Dulce Vista kitchen,
just the tip of the shit-berg. She may be
back with her dad now, but *Heavy* did *this* to her.

"I wanna help.

I can."
She means it, too—ready to fight for the truth.
Regulate on Heavy, karma boomeranging the king in the face,
right in the gold and white-gold grillz. Only right.
The monster GROANS, breaking up, turning.
Mel hopes he's considering. She goes on:

"You're not alone anymore.

I won't lose you again—"
Then she spots
collected human tongues mounted and displayed—
some cured, some fresh.
Raw.
Bloody.
The rawest pierced
with Kandela's stud
of a grinning skull.

Beneath them she sees the long, rusty shank; it drips

viscera.
Another Killa verse still playing:
> *"No need to stalk emcees—they see me comin'*
> *Know it's the end, no use to pretend, friend or victim, got*
> > *no choice*
> *Kill the noise, kill a voice, killa invoice*
> *Honey, throw on your gown, taking you out*
> *With funds from taking emcees out"*

"No…"
She draws away from him; the mask falls

from her hand.
> *"Hip-hop gonna save us, baby*
> *Write you more costume changes than Broadway legends*
> > *and bebop chords*
> *Change, Charlie Parker, leave 'em dizzy in a parked car*
> *Turning up the radio volume to bring a mockingbird*
> > *to life,*
> *Ode a nightingale to nirvana. Now you peep the level*
> > *I'm on*
> *Confident when I spit advice like*
> *be an emcee killa before an emcee kill ya*
> *Famous last words, forever quotable, if you prefer*
> *(this Ornithology is for the Birds)*
> *fertilizer-worth"*

The monster reaches for her, like: *Don't hate me…*
"No!"
> *"That's why I'm an emcee killa,*
> *I'm an emcee—"*

She recoils—

sees the monster struggle to understand.
He reaches for her again—

she wants to pity him, overstand, explain away—
but she can't.
Underworld only for the dead, Orpheus even failed;
world gone under for Mel, but…
She backs away.
Confusion in the monster's eyes.
He reaches for her one last time—
she slaps his hand away. Regrets it.
Sees his grotesque face boil—move from love
to the hate of being betrayed by the one
you love most.
He GROANS,
gutted, whatever human was left.
Oh. Shit.

       "Poe-ette?!"
Spur's voice—
the monster GROWLS.
Mel's panicked eyes dart past what-used-to-be her father, spot
a tunnel exit.
She looks at the monster,
sees her daddy in his expression—
a FLASH OF HER ORIGINAL HERO in better days
replaces the curse, a temporary concession.
But she can't leave him.
  Pretty-Dope feeling the pull of multiple directions, praying:
      Eleguá, 21-Faced god, don't leave me lost.
    Oshun, Virgin of Charity, wash me in the River of Clarity.
     Seriously, Yoruba Orishas and Catholic Saints,
      where you at now? Could really use your help.
A reading with seeds or shells, or a voice in her head—
  beggar ain't choosing. Missing her day one, Rosa,

and the blessings of Mima. Spur's voice straining to
    reach Mel:
        "Poe-ette?! Where you at?!"

The monster ROARS and spins toward the voice—vicious,
like Sid on steroids and lysergic acid diethylamide—a beast
erupting from its cage, volcano Vesuvius, killer of faith—
and Mel's back to her nightmare reality
in a Jack the Ripper alley, Victorian fog clogging her mind,
cogs in the machine turning like tarot cards, the Hanged Man
and Death. Mel like a canary in the coal-mine, sparrow
    landing
on a live line. Hearing her voice sound before she even decides:
    "Spur!"

Track 18

Lit

THE MONSTER SEIZES her—
she wonders: *to hold or to kill?*

Struggling to break loose, she wraps her fingers around a
lit candle.
Hits him with it, again and again.
It splits, flies out mid-swing—
across the cave—HITS another candle;
they FALL—
onto a trail of human detritus stretching through the tunnel
exit, like a fuse—
SPARK A FIRE—
burning note pads, notebooks, napkins—
Heavy posters, electronics, scavenged possessions igniting—
SPREADING…

10

Holy shit, she thinks as Spur rushes in from the tunnel
        and recoils:
            "Oh, shit!"
Freezes, axe in hand, what Mel glimpses
as she sees him struggle to gather his wits.

The monster snatches the long-shank
from under the severed-tongue stash.
Now!
And Mel gets free—
lunges for the tunnel, taking Spur with her.

                        ৶

Through the dank lower level,
her scuffed, blood-specked Adidas kicks on winged heels
as she flees through the dimness, still pulling Spur:
            "This way!"
He veers her past a fork, presumably the way he came.
She glances back. The monster rages out the cave.
Long-shank in its claws.
Mel follows the light cast from Spur's phone.
Not even slowing to get out her own.
Her first mentor turned minotaur.
SMOKE ENGULFING the path
behind the monster, obscuring him—
swallowed by the SMOG stalking them.
Mel turns forward, spots a LIGHT above
an
old
wooden

ladder
leading
up to a
long
shaft.

Like a beachhead for castaways cast adrift at sea,
sight for sore eyes, a site for eyes to soar and rise
up the rungs. Before they reach the base, a respite,
        "He's not following us,"   50
Spur says, then:
        "Holy shit! You okay?"
    "Are you?"
She hugs him, can't help it.
Presses her lips against his, passionate kiss,
genuine embrace. Just a taste, no time to waste—
    "I'm so sorry,"
has to share her regrets to repent, Mary Magdalene:
        "Forget about it," he says
—they release each other's waists, make haste toward the   60
    ladder, rungs in reach—
Mel excising a speech, beseeched:
    "I should've never let it keep going,
        should've never let you go back down either.
    You were right. This is all my fault."
Spur, always the gentleman:
            "Just worry about getting outta here.
            We'll work it out. I think we lost him."
Mel lost him a long time ago.
Her shell-toes advance toward the beachhead.   70
—BOOM—

the monster explodes out of the SMOKE
behind them—

    "Climb!"
Mel screams and pushes Spur up—
THE LADDER
Mel's sneakers just out of the monster's grasp—
she climbs—cracked, creaking step by step,
calling up to Spur as splinters stab her palms:
    "Hurry! Faster!"   80
Hears him calling back with a view of his ascending ass,
axe slung around his back:
        "I know! C'mon!"
Mel getting her bearings,
barely gaining distance, sharing airspace
with the monster behind her. Gaining up the ladder.
Terrified, she looks down—
just as a rung SNAPS
and the ladder shatters, GIVES WAY
under her   90
Adidas
—(hitting the monster)—
Her feet dislodge, swing free
over a fall
into
darkness—

    "Poe-ette!"
She hears Spur's scream descend past her
as she clings to the next step,
surprised she's still intact.   100

She hollers:
    "Keep flowin'! Go!"
Pulls herself up—straining—
ribs sore, elbows hurting, knees banged up,
ankles throbbing—next thing she knows,
she's being pulled up by Spur,
emerging from a manmade manhole
somewhere in the maze, yin and yang shadows stretching.
    "Don't say, 'I think we lost him again,'"
Mel says. Spur replies:
        "I won't."
Gasping, she hears the monster's FOOTSTEPS.
BOOTS STOMPING. STILL COMING.
    "Fuck a shit. Must know another way."
Home-field advantage ain't hers or Spur's.
Dashing, they take a wrong turn:
        "Where the fuck?"
    "This ain't the way from before."
        "We're lost. Gotta go back."
    "We can't!"
After another skidding turn, they reach a dead end.
Go through the only door—marked "TRAP ROOM" of
    all things—
into a storage room, crunching on roaches,
she spots a rust-hinged trap door in the ceiling—
    "That way!"
Spur says as Mel HEARS
THE BOOT-STEPS GETTING CLOSER.
She snatches her pretty boy by the cardigan, hurries
him past stacked music stands and equipment
leading to a mountain of stacked instruments

and some other shit.
Spur pushes her onto the steps, covers her back.
        "You first."
Mel climbs up to the door in the ceiling, leading. Unhooks
a rusty latch. Strains—no go—sealing their fates.
Mel like:
    "Fuckin' open!"
Feeling weaker with every failed attempt, going again—*shit!*
No use.
    "We need to switch!"
Hears Spur say:
        "Don't give up! I'll hold him off!"
    "What?"
Turns back, sees Spur block the monster's path
to her, raise the axe:
        "Just stay the fuck back!"
The monster lunges, dodges Spur's swing—unleashes
the long-knife—slices
Spur's throat in one motion; blood sprays—
Mel like:
    "NO!"

Track 19

Chiaroscuro

SPUR HITS THE ground
like spilled water.
Motionless,
open eyes set forward. Ready for pennies or silver sixpence,
the ferry costs Charon's obol.
Oh, no. Young and dead. Yorubas
would call this shit-predicament osogbo.
Voice in Mel's head like: *I gotta go—*
but I can't. Or won't. Don't know.

The monster slows.
What's he doing?
He's taking Spur's tongue.
No,
no,

no,
no,
no.
Witnessing, listening to the horror:
a sick sucking sound, rusted tearing,
jagged cutting, carving sinew   20
—a ruthless tug—
rip of flesh.

The monster steps over him,
bloody organ in hand, advances,
like he no longer recognizes his daughter.
Mel pushes harder against the rusted hinges.
Only now hears the QUAD FROM ABOVE,
THUMPING,
was being DROWNED OUT BY HER HEART.
Senses the sonic disturbance   30
as the monster reaches the steps,
within touching distance—reaching out,
when Mel extends a hand
to a mountain of stacked equipment, tips it—
it TOPPLES over the monster,
buys her a moment—maybe just an instant.
She strains harder, forces
the trap door
open,
and emerges   40
onstage.

Terrified and traumatized,
Mel SLAMS the hatch back down,

finds herself bathed in light.
The audience quiet, staring faces in the front.
She wipes hot sweat from her eyes,
sees she's interrupted a coronation.
Heavy placing the prize around V@$T @ppe@l's neck:
Raw-Y'all Records Jesus piece
—Mel's holy grail—or at least it used to be.   50

Ceremony frozen. Eyes on her.
All waiting for someone else to decide what's next.
Mel in a fugue state, smashed up. Hexed.
The crowd MURMURING.
Amazed-face, vexed, Heavy begins to play it
for the fans' benefit. Takes Mel by the arm:
　　"Sorry, hon.
　　You two rounds late
　　and your luck's run out.
　　Go wait backstage   60
　　for your consolation prize."
Crowd's voices a chorus, rejoicing, coming through like:
　　　　　　　　"ONE MORE ROUND!"
　　　　　　　　　　"ONE MORE ROUND!"
As the CHANTS CONTINUE, the words spark
something in Mel's eyes,
but it's not the high
of adoration.
A beast of another kind.
The stink of raw and rotted severed tongues   70
stuck in her nose overpowering the weed smoke.
Frees herself from his grip. About to let it rip.
The CHANTS CEASELESS,

CEASELESS,
CEASELESS—
She sees Heavy read the room. He improvises,
stuns V@$T @ppe@l by removing the Raw-Y'all Jesus piece
from his neck, and turns to her:
    "You hear 'em, Mellow-Dee.
    Maybe it ain't too late
    for you yet."
At the crossroads, Robert Johnson with the devil,
Eve with the snake. She knows what it means.
False king
aiming to do to her the same thing he did
to her dad. Turn her into a monster, cold
blooded killa begot by cold blooded killa,
ain't nothing realer, ain't nothing iller.
V@$T @ppe@l protesting, like: "What the shit? Fuck this
    bitch, dawg!"
Sick of tricks, Mel commandeers the mic, lets the drunken
    meter flow:
      "Listen now, understand later:
      I'm budding, strutting, jutting like a skyscraper
      Cutting capers of selling soul for love, hearts, and paper
      Post it, make it public, count the views later
      The lady sung mad wild, like a tongue
      With a lit fuse and a goal for now, not later"
Paces the stage, owning it, spotlight following.
In the clamshell footlights, sees SMOKE SEEPING
from below. Ain't fazing her.
Courage from Changó, knowledge from Orunmila.
      "No more abuse,
      Infringing copyright use,

Punk moves
Time to state rules"
Shining like the chandelier, finished taking it in the rear,
she sees Heavy can't take his eyes off of her. Digging it.
But dude could be seeing her in a halo of gold,
wouldn't matter: 110
> *"Life is what you make it, so*
> *Ain't no reason to fake it, 'cuz*
> *One day, somethin' will take it away*
> *How you wanna shake it down*
> *Break it down*
> *The pattern?*
> *Gotta think big*
> *Like Saturn*
> *Transcend on this plane of impermanence*
> *Turn a phrase rigged to sink shots*   120
> *In big shots*
> *And be great*
> *Like it was fate*
> *To matter"*

Savor the moment for a stolen instant.
Take a mental picture:
legendary image in the making,
like the Beatles crossing Abbey Road
and Dondi tagging subway walls. On the cusp;
Suffragettes, Gilgamesh, Malala;   130
Sumerian High Priestess Enheduanna,
the first author poet. Then fuck it:
> *"So here it is, and goes:*
> *I claimed 'emcee killa'*
> *When other words wouldn't give me they names*

Claimed 'emcee killa'
When flows became deserted like desert lakes
Claimed 'emcee killa' because it's what daddy used to say"
She sees Heavy put it together. He snatches the mic
    from her— 140
But there's no more fear or awe in her mind.
She goes a cappella—dropping her rhymes on him;
the Muse's lips kissing the tips of her ears,
tongue a stylus of the righteous.
    "Years ago, King Heavy took my old boy's life:
    His dreams, his biz, his rhymes
    His life force of àṣẹ
    In time
    Monetized his strife
    And tears 150
    Me and Mima paid the price
    I'm here to make things right"
Feel the heat, from underneath, steaming,
hot music given new meaning
as SMOKE CONTINUES SEEPING
FROM BELOW THE STAGE.
Everyone so focused on her,
they don't seem to notice a thing.
Must be attributing it to smoke machines
getting it on while she goes on: 160
    "Expose a demigod as a deadly fraud
    On a throne not his own that he stole
    Shitting lies on the microphone
    Crown deserving of higher ground
    H play ya like a fool, a tool
    Sell ya it's all cool

Well, I'm through
People, believe me if you feel me,
Know I just want y'all to see light clearly—
And hope you note I'm spittin' nothin' but truth　　　　170
For you,
Dearly—
To cope.
Sincerely,
Pretty-Dope"

The gathered don't seem to get it.
But they're recording on their phones.
Interest piqued to the peak.
Heavy seizes her:
　　"Ungrateful bitch—"　　　　180
when she hears
an EAR-PIERCING RUST-SQUEAL,
and glances up
as the SPEAKER-RIGGED CHANDELIER
comes loose—
　　　　one side—
　　　　　　　　then the other—
　　　　　　　　　　　　　　falls
　　"Watch out!"

The crowd barely scatter before it S H A T T E R S—　　　　190
CRUSHING everyone under it—
glass, debris, sparks flying—SHOCKWAVES reverberating
　　back to Mel;
she springs free from Heavy

as he and others shield themselves from
        RICOCHETING wreckage.
Seeing others drop from Deco-shrapnel hits,
Sweet Lady Jane, Truth-Is—two victims—
on the downside of trending.
The mom-and-pop Cuban chaperones and sons
in Nike suits, too. Escaped the Revolution, but not this.
Then she spots
the tongueless bodies
of 1DaFull,
Lil Bone-A-Part,
and Kandela Del Fuego,
tied to the center beam atop the carnage.

Mel choking on the gross truth of what it all means.
Oh, God…
Supernatural evil, might as well be.
The stage erupts into chaos, FLOODED BY SMOKE.
Caught in the panic, she looks for the nearest escape—
sights it beyond the crowd
OBSCURED BY SMOKE
when the monster EMERGES
FROM THE TRAPDOOR.

The Broken Night of the Vengeance

MEL WITNESSES V@$T @ppe@l fall
backward, fumbling for his pocket-knife.
Palpitating-ticker ride, fulla strife.
The monster wraps the back of V@$T @ppe@l's chain
around his ripped forearm—tightens it.
Mel backs away
as the SHARP TIPS
of the rose gold and diamond "V@$T @ppe@l" pendant
    PRESS into his throat—
rhinestones on his grill glinting as he vocalizes pain
    in baritone—
PIERCE through—gusher, plasma sprays
as V@$T falls dead onto the stage throne,

short-lived prince.
Gotta get out of this place!
But the herd are stampeding the doors—unable to get
     'em open.
Chaos—when Mel spots the rust-edged emergency exit map,
     iron staircase beside it.
Moonshot. New plot. *Gotta reach it—run!*
But she's drowning in a fog of fumes, CRASHING
into mic stands, turntables, the throne—coughing,
churning out smoke-induced tears, sight near useless—
until she grips the railing
and starts climbing the steps
to the roof exit—
when someone snatches her
by the neck—
Nicole Echo-No-Mics
pulling her away from the stairs,
silver hair disheveled, sans fedora:
     "Where's my son, bitch?"

Mel guilt ridden and anguished and fighting back—
sorry for Echo-No-Mics' son
but muthafuck his mom—
had to be in on what the king did to her dad:
          "Lemme go!"
But Echo-No-Mics pulls Mel farther from the stairs.
No one stopping or stepping to the king's sister,
known career killer, never work in this town again
if you cause her to frown—Mel resisting, seeing
               Nicole Echo-No-Mics' features up close, in
                    the carnage and the smoke:

curve of lips, corners of eyes, skin under
her throat,
one good eye tired, the other scarred.
"Where is my fucking son, you little bitch?!"
Suddenly the LONG-KNIFE pokes through—
blade-tip cutting air close to Mel.
BLOOD gurgles from Echo's mouth…   50
She squeezes her grip on Mel, then releases it—
as the long-shank retracts, and Nicole Echo-No-Mics drops.
The monster wielding the dripping knife.

Mel starts back toward the steps—
Don't glance back. Don't glance back.
Fuck. Closing in.
Why'd you look? Why'd you look? Told you not to—
POP!

She sees the monster shot in the arm.
Hears herself SCREAM—tastes the gulp   60
of burlap smoke scratch her throat. She sees—

Heavy with the gun. Versaces gone, eyes old:
cobwebs, crow's feet, red veins, capillaries, corneas. Shedding
     a tear
for his sister. Legendary boss left a husk,
from dust to dust. Heavy like:
     "Who the fuck—"

The monster turns from Mel to Heavy.
Bettino White stunned at the unmasked sight.
Overwhelmed,   70

like seeing a ghost. A phantom, a specter
blocking his exit, fire-singed.
Heavy whispers, choked up:
    "Apocalypse?"

The monster GROWLS, stalks away from Mel,
toward freaked Heavy, who's like:
    "You shouldn't be here.
    I had to do what I did.
    Kill or be killed, homie."
Heavy shoots, but the FLOOR STARTS TO GIVE,
QUAKES—
and he MISSES—drops the gun.
Monster unfazed, advancing.
Heavy on the ground, crying out:
    "Stop!
    You can still write for me!
    Or she can!
    I'll give her everything you wanted!"
He holds out his Cartier watch for a start.
The monster keeps coming.
Blade bloody. Mic stand in the other hand.
Like he wants to impale Heavy with the combo.
Mel can't leave it like this—
even as fire bleeds the theater dry.
Hears herself shout:
        "Stop! No more!"
The monster shoves her aside—
dead-set on Heavy, who finds the gun, fires off balance—POP!
Misses.
Unsteady, Heavy turns his gun on her.

The monster lets out a wet, gurgle-like cry.
She has no time before she sees the MUZZLE FLASH—
FIREWORKS POP!

Brace, clench, anticipate—check, scan for the pinch,
burn, numbness, warmth of liquid—
blood dripping out, leaking—all notions in an instant.
Unharmed, she sees the monster stagger—HIT
by Heavy's last shot, a wounded animal,
unable to help himself. Flames biting, searing.
Heavy flees up the stairs.   110

Mel has another chance to flee, instruments of escape play
    a symphony.
But…
She holds her hand out to the monster…
Come with me.

⅌

ON THE ROOFTOP,
short of breath, covered in sweat, blood and soot, Mel
emerges into the windy night, barely able
to help the monster stay stable. Flames pinching
her ass. Fuck the stench of rotten tongues,   120
gotta get dad home safe.

The lights of downtown haze in the distance
as she glances around in a desperate search—
past the FLICKERING "**VALDEMAR**" NEON
in the habañero squall.
SMOKE following them out—engulfing the rooftop

like the dancing-snake-smoke-tip of a cigarette,
wafting tendrils, flames licking out.
She sees the gooseneck fire escape stairs arcing over
the building's rear, hears the PANICKED CROWD   130
below.
She lugs her father toward the escape—
past the neon sign as it SHORTS and SPARKS out,
veiled by SMOKE, like words in fog.
And there's Heavy at the top of the fire exit,
calling out to her in the tempest:
        "Come with me! We can go places!"
POP! Heavy shoots her dad in the gut, shameless.
            "NO!"
Her papi staggers past her, growls like a dying animal.   140
Heavy doesn't give a shit:
        "Apocalypse with some fuckin
        wack-ass backpack raps.
        Serves you right."
POP, POP!
Heavy double-taps. Her father drops
to his knees—Mel tries to hold him up, but her fingers slip
in his blood. She falls beside him. Heavy like:
        "C'mon, kid, we need to roll.
        Fuck that old scrub.   150
        Heavy finna hook you up."
Magical words, the opportunity she coveted, price discounted.
Mission accomplished?
What it looks like on the razor's edge between dark and light.
Witching hour, wishes honored. *Wicked, huh?*
Mel's cold sweat running south her back to the crack,

chills of shame, self-doubt and loss slumming back up
     the track.
Puffing ash dragging her down. Emcee dragon tasting plasma.
Body bruised raw. Caught between the fire from below and the
     gust from above,
the Miami storm. Short of breath. Even less time to digest
     this mess.
Facts:
Heavy risking breath itself to make her sell out her own.
Tropical mistral about to call a mistrial on them all—
when she spots her dad's long-knife on the ground.
And hears MAD LAUGHTER SAMPLES
and BASS DROPS—
as a change creeps across
her consciousness…

Fact (like André 3 Stacks is the lyrical Hendrix, and perhaps
     now Kendrick).

View burning hot, orbit surrounded by ancestors and gods,
memories and thoughts, knowledge bound to be lost.
Heavy holds his hand out, rings fat with rubies and amethysts.
Mel sees his open fist—through the smoke storming like
     roaring clouds—
She stares up at her once-hero, contemplating his fate.
Turned him down before, but decision's now about war. And it
     can't wait.
Road-chasing windmills and waterfalls over the rainbow lead-
     ing her here, y'all.
Choosing between massacre and mercy. *Villain or hero, Mel?*
     Which one are you, boo?

Ain't too late to learn the truth.
Heavy saying:
    "You don't wanna miss out on this train,
    Mellow-Dee. Last chance.
    Goin', goin'…
    You hear?! I turned down
    deals with Aftermath and Def Jam
    just 'cuz I don't need 'em!
    Sure as shit don't need you either!
    Tryin' to do you a solid! Save you, bitch!
    Now, c'mon, stop fuckin' around and frontin'!"
Now, Mel nods to herself.
Dilemma solved.
Heavy like:
    "That's my girl."
Hairs on the back of her neck standing up, knowing
    what's next.
She rises with the blade,
    STABS him through the bag—
        feeling the resistance of flesh,
            pushing through it nonetheless—
                launches greenbacks into the wind—\$ \$ \$ \$
                    \$ \$ \$ \$
Making his eyes go Kandela-wide
in surprise—and the GRUNT-SQUEAL SOUND
that escapes him deep and profound.

Heavy looks to her, ruined. Disappointed.
The US kale going up—loose bills escaping—
He backs up, knife embedded. A grotesque sight—
but worth it.

False king shrinking, squeal receding to a falsetto echo.
Mel steps to the edge. Pulls the knife—
sees Heavy fall
off the roof;
he disappears
into the smoke
abyss, vanquished.

She turns back. *Where's Dad? Gotta help him.*
Hooks his singed, seared and blackened arm—straining
joints and limbs to keep him up,
struggling to help her true hero
to the fire escape; finally, start climbing down—
but her father shakes his head.
Steps back, red orbs saying, *"goodbye."*
What's he doing?
Holy fuck, no!—
as he tries to speak, a sound she can't discern—
A FIREBALL swallows him whole as the
    ROOF COLLAPSES,
                  IMPLODES
beneath him.
    "Daddy, NO!"

Down he goes—
time slowed, too painful—
his face more like the one in her childhood memories
than the abomination from this nightmare spree;
the hands that once did the *got-your-nose* trick
the last things she sees
before he's gone.

Nah, Nah, Nah—back that up.
Too late.
Fire and smoke are all that's left. Fast. Ambiguous.
Indifferent.
Part of her dying with him.
DJ-scratching, looping the recording before her irises.   250
Losin' it?
Nah, just seeing a killa justified.

Mel clinging to the fire escape.
Ablaze dawn aurora beginning to streak the cityscape with
spray paint.
Perfect alignment, circle round despite the haze.
It's too much. A tear bleeds
down her cheek, evaporates in the heat.
She shakes, losing it. Spigot. Roars a primal scream—
doesn't hear a sound.   260

Graced.

Track 21

Killa
(Outro)

FRANKLINS, HAMILTONS AND Jacksons float in the
dawn breeze—
   some bills burnt, others aflame, amount nothing to
sneeze at.
Morning warm. Mourning more. Salty beach sand in the mix.
Homeless peeps and late-nighters
going crazy for it—the bills, that is—
Benjamins and Lin-Manuels—
down the boulevard at daybreak.
Club Valdemar remains
in spirit alone—pancaked, smoke-cloaked ruins.
Fractured neon sign sparking live wires
atop the burial mound, ensnared in the mangled rebar.

Sirens earsplitting, muted down to a whisper. Bruised
clouds brooding above, waiting to pounce, transmitting.

Moving through the dehydrated,
drained survivors, spent from after-hours beyond the bargain,
in one hand, a water bottle;
Miles, the fish, still swimming
at her side as Mel carries the 24-ounce by the cap and neck,
limping with a stagger
through the cash cloud,
letting it STIR IN THE WIND…
                    $ $ $ $ $ $
Eyes fixed forward
at nothing
and everything.
Freestyling:
    "Whether happened or fiction
    That's my story
    Lost money but hit the blood lottery
    Jackpot!
    Lost dad, lost shot, lost all I got
    Time to go home to mom
    Deal with life's ka-booms, busts and bombs
    Try to stay
        Calm…
          Make peace with Mima"
One Adidas missing.
Snap the other off, with no ankle socks,
bare feet hot on the concrete beach.
Lotus flower that grew from the locust cracks—gorgeous.
Gotta dance, dance, dance.

Keep on grooving to the polyrhythmic beat.
Songs in the key of heat.
She—no—*fuck a third person*—
I mean: I,

       I,

         I,

Pretty-Dope, Bonita Dopeness, Melody—   50

                          I—

the storyteller,
unfurling the yarn—
Me,
the scribe, the singer, the bard, the author,
the star for all to see—
We,
the collective bacterias and synapses
that constitute me—
your humble narrator,
limping with swagger.   60
Spitting truth for you,

           you,

              you.

Heavenly fruit juice, boo.
No more shame, no more stage fright, no more fear
of failure, of being lame—of anything
(guilt, that's a separate thing).

Way it's gotta be.

Fly like Childish Gambino clad in Valentino. Awaken,
    My Love.   70

As survivors scramble around me
to catch bills stirring in the breeze—

$ $ $ $ $ $

—bumping, jumping,
running into the street—CARS
CRASHING behind the scenes, candy paint Maseratis—
doubters gonna hate, and haters gonna doubt,
scheming up is down, and down is up,
trying to hide spines,
trying to kill dreams—
my dreams, your dreams—
Madam, I'm Adam palindrome.
Esteemed Muse, listen,

listen,

listen—

Forgive 'em.
   Enlightened:
        all gonna die, all more alike,
        souls seeking control,
        converging cosmic roads,
        all one energy pulse,

pulse,

pulse,

anima mundi,
into the Unknown,
until this chord progression resolves itself;
empath now, feeling it all. You are not alone.

Forget 'em.
Sunbeams shining full lightbulb moons upon me

and you, and our brave blade too.
Such small things—fragile, precious—really.   100
Weep at the beauty. A vision. A blessing on its own.
Essential life force of àṣẹ. Seeds growing.

Fuck 'em.
Pedestrians part for Moses, see me cross through
like I'm rolling with a music vid crew.
I drop my hoodie,
keep the chin high.
In my other hand, Daddy's long-knife—
not even barely concealed up the sleeve at my side.
No time for secrets. Letting it ride.   110
Heart on your sleeve, way it's gotta be.
Blood on the blade sticky, crimson caramel,
iron-rust smell like a tab of acid gel—
I could get into this,
like what Daddy did, but my own thing.

Way it's gotta be.

Got a new playlist—here's just the tip of it:
—Greg, Mima's fuck-buddy boss, who digs my lips
on his biz—and that ain't it;   120
—How 'bout Art, Mima's ex who slipped me X,
tripped into me next,
no permission, no 'yes,' no lube, no jimmy—raining,
    no umbrella—
read the rest:
—Those wannabe bangers that jacked me on the metro, bust
    back at those busters from the bus;

—Asshole dude who cut Mima's Civic off and flashed a gun,
    road-raging;
—Dirty politicians; corrupt interests; crooked cops;   130
    animal abusers;
fashionable skeptics; the willful ignorant; cold-blooded killers;
    self-righteous sinners.
Could go on and on:
—The ex-first love who broke my heart, stroke of pain
    still sharp,
Thou Who Shall Remain Nameless;
—And even *you*—
Dear Listener, Esteemed Muse,
not blameless,   140
if you don't heed these freestyle truths
on this mixtape of memories, murders, and myths;
plenty deserving
slit wrists, throats, tongues, lips,
all the rest. Just the tips of the list.
Unfinished business.

Shout-out to EPMD.

Way it's gotta be.

That's the Biz. Read the marquee.

I know what you're thinking, but just listen.   150

Pedestrians flash stares like I'm crazy—
(know what I think)—
American Dream

as they chase paper around me—

$ \$ \ \$ \ \$ \ \$ \ \$ \ \$ $

I just keep on…
    "Flowing:
    So the old boss can take a loss
    Give him head?
    No, take his head instead
    Oh, to be young and ready for Greg—
    Or Art the Prequel—
    'Cuz few emcee 'round here left to bring it in they stead
    Help my cause, fill my needs
    You see?
    Long-knife handle be mad sticky
    And blade hungry to feed
    Blowing out this damn spot
    Way it's gotta be"
Into the thick Miami dawn,
ancestors and Orishas walking with.

Even Day One Rosa by my side, in her prom dress
with a live round in her abdomen, rocking a proud smile.
    "'Cuz ain't none illa,
    ain't none reala…"
Spur, too, in a sky-blue cardigan,
throat still slit, tongue still gone—gonna have to work
    around shit.

As survivors scramble around me,
Esteemed Muse, listen,
                        listen,
                    listen—

I just gotta keep on going, growing, flowing, swimming, lift-
    ing, ripping the roof off the street,
singing:
    "I'm an emcee killa,
        I'm an emcee killa,
            I'm an emcee—"

Shout-Outs

(The author would like to thank)

THE HEART

Maria, the Realest, the Woman—my wife, rock, frequent inspiration—who encouraged me for years to take the plunge and write the book I kept saying I wanted to write. As usual, you were right.

THE FAM

My mother, Caridad Vasquez, my first favorite storyteller and biggest influence (RIP). My father, Mario Edison Moreno, my first editor—for all the knowledge and support. Brothers Archie and Juan Alberto (John) Hernandez, for teaching me about music, dedication, and the value of practice during Afro-Cuban jazz jam sessions every night in our house on Sedgwick in the Bronx. Estefanie Morena, sister and forever muse. Sister-from-another-mother, Tanja. Beloved niece, Luna. Cousins Gabe, Frankie, Doug, Omar, and David. The Moreno family—all aunts, uncles, stepmoms, cousins, partners, kids, and pets. Special shout-outs to Susan & Jaime Moreno, for an incalculable amount of support. Tio Rey, for the camcorder. Great-grandad

Alejandro Moreno Jr. (the war reporter and playwright), and his sisters, the teachers. The Rodriguez, López, Canosa, and Muñoz families. Ancestors: those unknown—everyone that had to have sex so I could be here. Bisabuela Rossi (maternal great-grandma—who taught my grandfather the piano—the farthest back we can trace our family's love of music). My departed older brothers, Mario and Eric, and my lost sister, Amor.

EVOL KNOWN ARTISTS AND ASSOCIATES (MIAMI)

Robert O'Neill, Leins Nome Rios, Luis H. Rodriguez, Johnny Bland, Jason Padaetz, Nicolay Adinaguev, Erik Martens, Phillip Berdoll. And all the brothers and sisters from other mothers. EKA Crew+ (see *Graffiti Labyrinth*). BHP: Bay Harbor Posse. IBS: Infamous Blunt Squad. RMS Crew: Rocking Miami Streets w/ Real Mad Stylez (circa '95-'99). Beach High Hi-Tides. Florida State Thespian Troupe 391. Mrs. Diez' Dark Room Collective. Nautilus Sharks. Normandy Pictures. DADE WEAR. Trifekta Studios. FRAME DEFENDER. Miami Grill. Empower Lift. Blockbuster. BTW Crew. Le New York. 94th and 95th St., 88th, the Island, 7-1, 64th-65th, 85th, 123rd, NMB, South Beach, Surfside, Sunset Island, Eastern Shores, Hallandale, Hollywood, Lauderdale, Aventura, Miami Gardens, Hialeah, the Grove, Wynwood, and all points in between. Antonio De La Cruz for the influence. And Lenny Rein for the recommend.

THE TEACHERS

Florence, flute instructor and English tutor back in '86. Pat, who used to read us Poe in kindergarten at Barnard School in the Heights (RIP). Diane Davidowitz, the Barnard admin who so patiently helped us write a play in 2nd grade, and Janet Olsen, our music appreciation teacher. The Oluwos, who taught me the ways of Ifá. And, the teachers at Bay Harbor Elementary: Mrs.

Putney, Miss Thomas, Mr. Grim, Mrs. Turner, (Miss Barros). Mr. Purvis at Nautilus. The nurturers of creativity at Miami Beach Senior High (95-99) and beyond. The Great Gary A. Graff (for changing the course of my life), Christopher Dreeson (for Gatsby, Hitchcock, and Poe), Carmen Junquera-Diez (for the rule of thirds, go closer, and go darker), Tom Virgin (for being cool). The MIU Crew: Tara Huynh, John Huynh, Frank Longo, Ernest Goodly, John Mass, Jason Rodgers, Sam Beam (Iron & Wine), Alvaro Bertrand, Yahr, Norris. And my students, who taught me as much as anyone.

THE WESTCYDE

Andy's Writers Group: including Andy Guerdat (for his incalculable contribution), Anthony Grieco, Lily Dahl, Bryan Roy, Katiedid Langrock, Kay Tuxford, Sadie Dean, Henry Dunham, Lauren Fash, Adi Blotman, Jeff Drongowski, Soo Jin Hwang, Nick Brandt, Italome Ohikhuare, Chris Retts. And Write Club: Jeff Stoltzfus, Sam Simkin, Pete D'Alessandro, Ross Sauriol. Cousin Juli Moreno (Wild Optimists). Dana Hahn (the Connector). Micki Grover. Elena Grieco. Jesse Douma. Ryan Kelley. Anne Marie Boidock. Palak Patel. Bryan Barber. Corey Ball. Gabriel Savo. Catherine McNulty. Brentano's Bookstore in Century City: Meesha Dibner, Howie Blakeslee, Hyo-Mi Pak, Adi Cornejo, Bill Rupel, Asya Dobbins, Irene Yeung, Erik Frost-Barnes, Robert Maitia, Roger Stover, Brian Martin, Harry, Gio, and the rest of the old school crew. Maggie Roiphe, Mark Yellen, for believing in this project. Giovanni Ribisi. Mary Krell-Oishi. Mark Hamilton. John Orland. Joe Beatty. John and Stefania Luxenberg. The Valentines. The Coolers. Our Hospitality. Miguel Ortega (305 to 310). Adam Randall. Ricardo de Montreuil. Jeanne Veillette Bowerman. Danny Manus. Richard "RB"

Botto. Matt Dy. Doug Amaturo. Annalisa Koukouves. Nicky Weinstock. Breean Solberg. Aimee Rivera. Bill Borden. Skip Woods. Guymon Casady. Karen Wyscarver, Sanford Golden. Marc Canter. The LA Series team (for what could've been): Iris Torres, James Franco, Pedro Gomeź Millán, Carlos Bardem, Esai Morales, Eva Tamargo, Manu Rulfo, Chelsea Rendon, Vanessa Villela, Daniel Moncada, Didda Scheving, and all the cast and crew. Also, McKuin Frankel Whitehead LLP. Iliad Books. Dark Delicacies. The Last Bookstore. Amoeba Music. Atomic Records. Freak Beat. The Arclight. The WGA. The Writers Store. BJ Markel, Save The Cat! Script Mag. AFF. Joe Jarvis, Shelly Mellott, and the entire Final Draft family (past and present).

THE EDITOR
Special thanks to Kerry Cullen for keeping me honest. All errors are my own.

THE INSPIRATIONS +
Influences as inspiring in-person: Gabriel García Márquez, André 3000, Nic Pileggi, Slimkid3, Fatlip, Imani (of the Pharcyde); De La Soul, "Captain" Kirk (thanks for the Fallon tix!) and Questlove from the Roots (thanks for not kicking us out of the dressing room/recording studio!). Sidney Poitier, Jean-Pierre Jeunet, Michael Connelly, Khalid Hosseini, Robert Crais, Gregg Hurwitz, Robert Masello, Wendy Calhoun, James Elroy, William Goldman, Shane Blank, Steven Zaillian, Paul Dini, Bruce Timm, Chris Rock, Glen David Gold, Chuck Palahniuk, Carl Gotlieb, Anthony Kiedis, Nas, Kelis, Malcolm McDowell, Al Pacino, Faye Dunaway, Ali Shaheed Muhammad, Talia Shire, Meg & Lawrence Kasdan, Vince Gilligan, Margot Kidder, Mick Foley, Carl Weathers, Keith David, Sam Raimi, Richard Dreyfuss,

Todd Field, Johnny Pacheco, Diana Ross, Walter Murch, Ridley Scott, Harlan Ellison, Vivian Kubrick, and James B. Harris.

THE REST-IN-PEACE VIPS
Cristobal "Pilly" Alvarado (my first creative collaborator), Los Abuelitos, Tia Martha, Tio Enrique, Tia Mercedita. Mogambo el Indio, El Guerrero, Pedro Perrin, Miguel Febles, Tata Gaitán, Agapito Piloto, Mario Mendoza, Rob Williams, Elton Sebastian, Blake Snyder, Syd Field, Kulayed, Roberta Rodriguez, and the full Mojuba.

THE MEOWS
Melanie, Missy, & Midnight, (for all the mystery).

And thank you, Dear Reader.

Love & cheers

About the Author

MARIO MORENO is a Cuban Colombian American author, screenwriter, coach, and former graffiti artist, Bronx-born, Miami-raised. The grandson of legendary bandleader Belisario López, Mario dreamt of playing the bass. But his father went to prison for crimes involving the White House and the mob, and 

Mario ended up writing noirs about the American Dream. He's crafted stories for Sony's Columbia Pictures, Rabbit Bandini, and the National Institute of Cinema and Audiovisual Arts (INCAA), among others. He's also the Product Manager for Final Draft, driving the design and development of the industry-standard screenwriting software while advocating for storytellers and content creators. *KILLA*, adapted from his Austin Film Festival finalist script, is his dark love letter to hip-hop and gothic horror. He lives in Los Angeles with his family.

www.mariomorenowrites.com
Twitter: @MarioOMoreno37
IG: @MarioMoreno37

www.ingramcontent.com/pod-product-compliance
Lightning Source LLC
Chambersburg PA
CBHW031035310726
48969CB00007B/1994